THE SECRETS
OF THE
CRYSTAL GEM

LUCY KHAN

All correspondence to the author:
khanlucy2016@gmail.com

© Copyright Lucy Khan

First Printed in Australia, 2025

Cover artwork by Miblart.

Reference:
The Holy Bible, New International Version® NIV®
Copyright © 1973, 1978, 1984, 2011 by Biblica, Inc.®
Used by Permission of Biblica, Inc.® All rights reserved worldwide.

The right of Lucy Khan to be identified as the author of this work
has been asserted by her in accordance with the Copyright,
Designs and Patents act. All rights reserved.

ISBN: 978-0-646-71418-9

Proudly produced by

TheBookStudio

www.thebookstudio.com.au

*To Kelly, Larissa, Isis, Jendy and Phil.
Thanks for your support, advice and help
with the creation of this book.*

*And to God, for everything he has done in my life.
Thank you.*

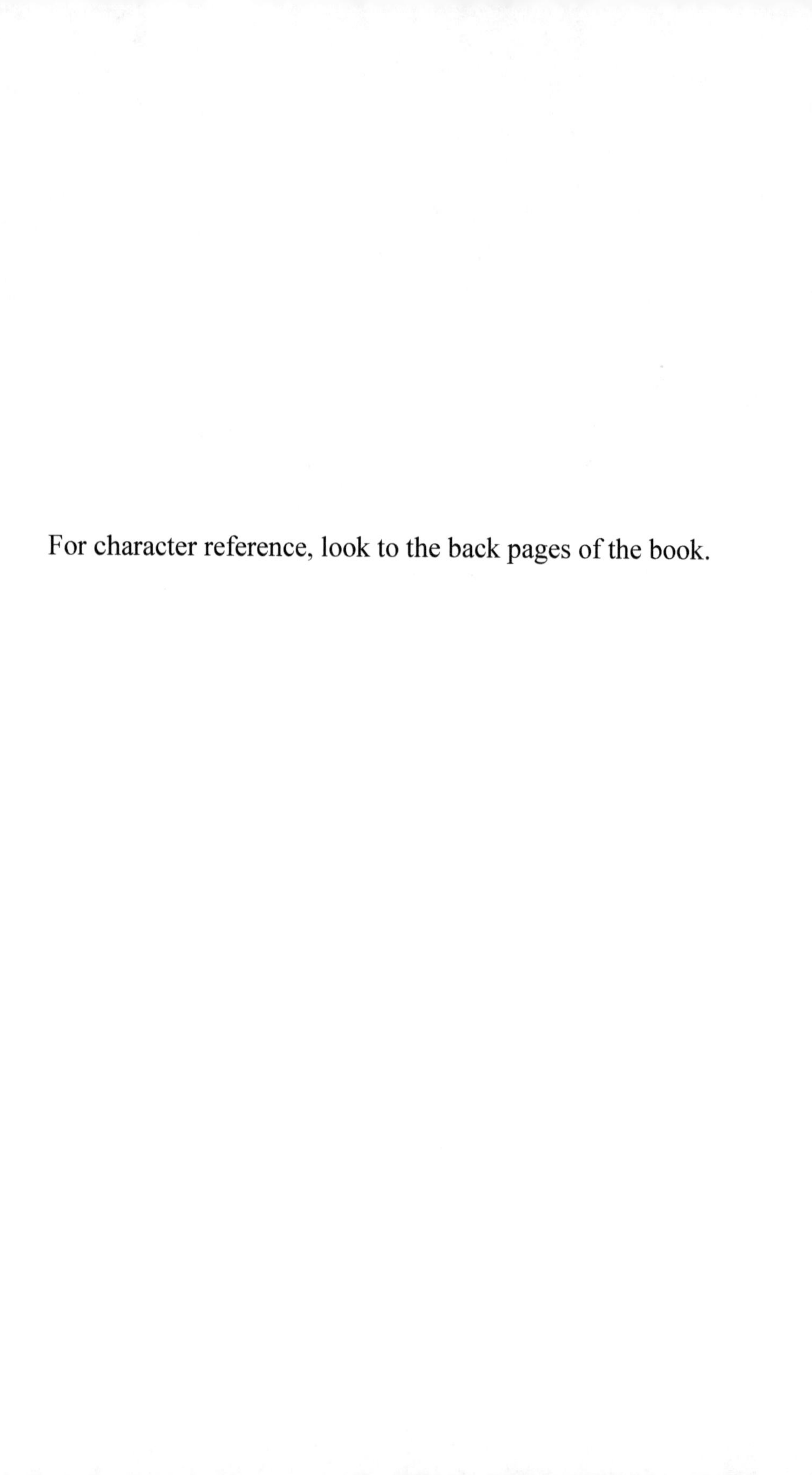

For character reference, look to the back pages of the book.

PROLOGUE

The Prince of Darkness was thrilled to finally see Claud back with the wagon full of victims, that he had gotten from Jorogumo. He was growing board with each hour, as he waited for his return. He was eager to have his strength back even if he was not at his fullest yet. After positioning the wagon in front of the Prince of Darkness, Claud bowed to his master and waited for further instructions, hoping he would not be ordered to see Jorogumo again.

"I have a mission for you Claud," The Prince of Darkness declared.

"Yes Master," Claud replied, bowing in front of him in relief.

"I need you to go to the Kingdom of Elaxon and get me the sapphire healing Gem. If you can't retrieve it from the Queen, find out where they buried the previous King and steal it from his grave. I need that Gem to help me get my full strength back," the Prince of Darkness growled. "Do not come back until you have it."

"Yes Master," Claud said.

After bowing to his master again, Claud stood up and left the cave of Akuma smiling to himself. He would finally have his revenge on Issac for killing his beloved friend Selina. After transforming into a massive wolf, he ran into the forest and headed towards the Kingdom of Elaxon.

CHAPTER ONE

"If either of them falls down, one can help the other up.
But pity anyone who falls and has no one to help them up."

Ecclesiastes 4:10

Finnick lay awake in his tent, staring at the roof. After they had defeated Jorogumo, the soldiers all came back to their campsite to celebrate their victory. But it was not a time for celebration for Finnick. He had lost his best friend Jarreth in the recent battle, and was in no mood to see anyone. Jarreth had been like a brother to Finnick, both finding enjoyment in pranking their Captain when they were younger. This made Captain Oberon a father figure to them both. Captain Oberon had taught him and Jarreth everything he knew. How to fight and stay alive. This is why Jarreth's death was so depressing and hard. He had not only lost a friend, but also a brother.

"Why?" Finnick spoke to the God of Light. "Why take my friend?"

Unable to sleep, Finnick got up, got dressed and went to train. He needed to keep his mind occupied until the King and Queen were ready to leave for their next mission. To locate the Crystal Gem that is supposed to be the Prince of Darkness's weakness. Anger surged through him as he thought about the Dark One.

Finnick stepped out of his tent and had to shield his eyes from the bright morning sun as his eyes adjusted. The lack of sleep did not help either, so he made his way over to the food tent. After accepting a cup of coffee from one of the staff, he walked over to the usual training area where he, Lucas and Jarreth used to train for hours at a time. Walking over he saw Lucas already up and training with Jarreth's bow and arrow. Finnick could not use Jarreth's weapon and knew it would be used more if Lucas owned it instead. That was why he gave it to Lucas instead of keeping it. When Lucas finished shooting all the arrows into the tree, he walked over and took them all out to shoot again. Upon walking back, he noticed Finnick watching him.

"Morning Finnick," Lucas said with indifference.

"Hey buddy," Finnick said patting his head "Why are you up so early?"

"Couldn't sleep. You?" Lucas asked.

"Yeah, me neither," Finnick said watching Lucas shoot his arrows.

"You've gotten good," Finnick praised, watching Lucas shoot.

"Thank you," Lucas replied, looking at the bow sadly.

"Finnick, Lucas," said a gruff voice behind them.

"Captain," Finnick greeted, shocked to see his Captain up so early.

"Couldn't sleep either?" Oberon asked them both.

"No," they both replied sadly.

Oberon nodded looking at them both. He could understand their pain and sadness but was not particularly good at comforting people.

"Coffee?" he asked.

"Sure," Finnick said, looking at his now empty cup. "I could go with another."

"I've never tried it," Lucas said.

"Well lad, it's your lucky day," Oberon said.

Finnick gestured to Lucas to follow him, as Oberon led them over to the food tent. After waiting in line for a few minutes, they were finally served by Dottie, who greeted them with a warm smile.

"Morning lads," Dottie said cheerily. "Coffee?"

"Three please, milk and one sugar please," Oberon ordered.

"I know you're a big muscular fellow, but isn't three a bit much?" Dottie asked eyeing Oberon up and down.

Oberon moved aside, and Dottie saw Finnick and Lucas standing behind him looking gloomy.

"Well, that makes more sense," Dottie said, writing up the order.

Once Dottie had finished making the coffee's, she handed them over to Oberon.

"Here you go Captain," Dottie said, giving Oberon the cups.

"Thanks," Oberon said, turning to give the coffee's to Finnick and Lucas.

Finnick took his with a smile and began drinking straight away despite it being piping hot, while Lucas looked at the cup in his hand. He brought the cup up to his nose and sniffed it.

"Smells okay," Lucas said.

"It's heaven in a cup," Oberon said savouring the taste.

Oberon then walked over to a table and sat down, Finnick and Lucas followed him, and they all drank their coffee in silence.

"Can I come with you guys on the next mission?" Lucas asked unexpectedly. "I've practiced my knife throwing and archery, and I'm really, really good."

Finnick and Oberon looked at each other.

"It's dangerous Lucas," Finnick began.

"I know, but I'm good, you said so yourself Finnick," Lucas begged.

"Lad, this mission is dangerous," Oberon stated. "Plus, I think Queen Athena and Princess Iris will need your help here, with restoring your home."

"Okay," Lucas mumbled in defeat.

"Morning Captain Oberon, Finnick, Lucas," Omari greeted. "How did you all sleep?"

"Okay," Lucas said sipping his coffee.

"Not much," Finnick said, as he let out a huge yawn.

"Yeah okay, what about you Prince Omari?" Oberon asked.

"Yeah, I managed to finally fall asleep after Queen Juliet gave me some valerian root," Omari explained.

"Dammit, I should have asked for some too," Finnick said, feeling stupid for forgetting.

"We can ask her tonight, I'll remind you," Omari reassured.

"Thanks Prince Omari," Oberon said, managing a half smile despite being exhausted.

"Appreciate it," Finnick said, hiding his yawn behind his hand.

"Prince Omari," Dottie called, coming up with a bag.

"Supplies for the travelling company," Dottie said. "Good luck in your quest." She smiled before walking off.

"Thank you," Omari called back.

"Is the King and Queen awake?" Oberon asked.

"Yes, they are saddling up their horses as we speak. We all had a quick breakfast of nuts and fruits, as King Nikolai thought it was best to leave soon to find the Gem," Omari explained.

"Good call," Oberon said standing up. "We best be over there helping, Finnick."

"Yes sir," Finnick replied, patting Lucas on the head before getting up and following his Captain.

Captain Oberon made his way over to Nikolai who was busy attaching multiple bags to his horse.

"Morning Your Highness," Oberon greeted.

Nikolai turned to see Oberon and Finnick behind him still looking half asleep.

"Morning Captain, Lieutenant Finnick," Nikolai greeted, staring at them both with concern. "It does not look like either of you have had much sleep. It's understandable, but remind myself or Juliet and we can give you some valerian root tonight to help."

"Thanks, appreciate it, Your Highness," they both replied, then smiled tiredly.

"What can we do to help?" Oberon asked.

"Get your horses ready, then we can divide the rest of the packing up," Nikolai suggested.

Oberon nodded "Of course."

Oberon and Finnick went to find their horses, which were tied to a post nearby eating grass. Upon their approach, the horses' heads shot up and sniffed at their familiar owners. Finnick chuckled and patted his horse's nose. His horse was a dark chestnut brown with patches of white on its body. "It's good to see you again Bucky."

Finnick's horse neighed loudly, stopping its foot on the ground.

Finnick turned around and saw Iris walking by. After beckoning her over he asked her to interpret why his horse was moody. She looked just as exhausted as he felt. Loosing Jarreth and her father must have taken a toll on her as well.

"What did he say?" Finnick asked curiously.

"He's asking where you've been," Iris interpreted. "But with a bit more enthusiasm."

"Oh," Finnick said turning back to his horse. "Out fighting monsters. You would have hated it, giant spiders."

Bucky neighed and shook his head.

Finnick turned to Iris to interpret.

"Bucky said, nope, you're on your own with that one," Iris said, smiling a little.

Finnick turned back to his horse and patted his head.

"Yeah," was all he could say, as it brought back memories of losing his friend.

"You both have a good bond," Iris said patting Bucky's head.

"We've been together since I was 10. Dad brought him for me as a pony, we grew up together, been through many battles," Finnick said reminiscing.

"I'm sorry you lost your friend," Iris whispered, trying not to cry.

"I'm sorry you lost someone who cared for you," Finnick said sadly.

Bucky nuzzled his head on Finnick's shoulder for comfort, then did the same to Iris. Finnick patted his head, thinking to himself he was lucky to have Bucky as a horse. Iris patted Bucky's head and thanked Finnick before walking away, afraid she would break down in tears again.

"Your Highness, here is the list of things you requested," a solider said, coming up to Princess Iris with a box.

"Thank you," Iris replied, turning around to find Juliet with Amisha. "The contents of the box go to Queen Juliet." Iris pointed out Juliet to the soldier.

"Of course," the soldier replied, turning, and heading to Juliet.

"Your Highness," the soldier said, showing the box to Juliet.

"Oh, wonderful, thank you," Juliet replied.

The soldier nodded and walked away as Juliet rummage through the box finding what she needed.

"Yes, perfect," Juliet said holding up a bridle and saddle.

Amisha neighed and moved back shaking her head.

"Amisha, how can I ride you without a saddle?" Juliet asked.

Amisha neighed at Juliet, who stood dumbfounded at her

alicorn, as she could not understand her. Thankfully, Iris came up and stood beside Juliet to interpret.

"You can't expect the Queen to ride without a saddle, and with just your hair as a means to hold onto," Iris said to Amisha.

"Uh no, I cannot do that," Juliet agreed.

Amisha neighed and looked to the ground in defeat.

"How about we compromise," Juliet said lifting Amisha head up. "Just a saddle and no bridle."

Amisha neighed and nodded her head in approval.

"Great," Juliet said lifting the saddle. "I promise this one will be far more comfortable for your wings than the last one. Princess Iris asked a friend to adjust it especially for you."

While Juliet fitted the saddle onto Amisha, Omari produced a bag of supplies that Dottie has generously made up for them all.

"Queen Juliet," Omari greeted.

"Hello Prince Omari," Juliet said, as she finished strapping the saddle on.

"Supplies from Dottie," Omari said opening the bag. "A couple of water flasks, bread, cheese, nuts and fruit."

"Tell Dottie I said thank you," Juliet said, as she took the bag.

"Will do," Omari said walking off.

Nix came up to Amisha and sniffed her nose, then Amisha licked Nix's face causing Nix to bark playfully. Juliet smiled as she watched the two get along. Watching them play reminded her of her childhood days, as she played with the animals that she and Lacy had found. Some had been injured, and Juliet would use her healing abilities on them to help the animals before setting them free. She would then release them back into the wild with the help of Issac.

"Juliet," she heard her name being called.

"Hm." Juliet turned to find Nikolai watching her curiously.

"Are you okay?" he asked, coming up to hug her.

"Yes, just lost in thought," Juliet said, smiling at her husband.

"Nix has gotten along with Amisha quite well, hasn't he?" Nikolai observed.

"He has. It's cute how well they get along," Juliet said smiling as she watched Nix and Amisha play.

"Your Highnesses," Oberon said running up to them. "There's something you need to see."

Curious, both Nikolai and Juliet followed Oberon as he led them to Queen Athena's tent. Upon entering, they saw a vulture lying on the table all tied up and injured, its breathing was shallow as Juliet and Nikolai inspected the bird.

"What's going on?" Juliet asked.

"We believe it's a spy from the Prince of Darkness, and it's mission was to keep trailing us, until we found the Crystal Gem," Captain Chase reported.

"How do you know?" Nikolai asked.

"The fox who managed to persuade Mildred into changing sides," the vulture spoke up. "But you won't persuade me, I know where my allegiance lies."

"That's how," Chase said glaring at the vulture.

"What do you suggest we do with it?" Oberon asked.

Nikolai turned to Queen Athena.

"Do you mind holding it in your dungeons?" Nikolai asked.

"Not at all," Queen Athena said, turning towards Chase. "Captain, please take it to the dungeons."

"Oh course, Your Highness," Chase said, stepping close to the vulture.

"Wait!!!," the vulture screamed, trying to get loose.

"Thinking about changing allegiance?" Chase asked.

"Never," the vulture snarled.

"The dungeons it is," Chase said, reaching for the bird again.

"You can't put me down there, Jorogumo was just there. What

if her minions are still down there?" the vulture screeched.

"Not my problem," Chase replied.

The vulture screamed and struggled, as Chase took the bird out of the tent while the others stared from behind.

"Now I understand how the Prince of Darkness knows so much," Nikolai said, concerned.

"He must have been watching us this whole time," Oberon said.

"That means he knows that we know his weakness is the Crystal Gem," Juliet said worriedly. "His followers will be after us."

"True," Queen Athena spoke up. "But it also means that this Crystal Gem is powerful, for him to fear it so."

"Then we need to find it as soon as possible," Nikolai said determined.

"Everything is all ready for our quest," Iris said, coming through the tent.

"You're coming with us?" Oberon asked, surprised.

"Yes, I need the distraction, otherwise I will go insane. Plus, I want to help," Iris replied, standing ready, then looked towards her mother. "Please."

"Promise me you'll come back safe," Queen Athena replied, nodding her approval.

"Thank you, mother," Iris said, giving her a hug.

"Now that everything is ready, we may as well leave now. The sooner we find the Gem, the sooner we can end this war," Nikolai told the group.

The group nodded, showing that they were just as eager as he was to start the mission. One by one they all exited the tent and headed to their own horses.

"Be safe out there, I'll be praying to the God of Light for all of you," Queen Athena said, waving.

"Thanks mother," Iris said, hugging her once more before running back to the group.

When Iris left the tent, she saw everyone headed to their own horses, checking last minute that they had everything for the mission. But Iris did not want to ride her horse. Her mother would need all the extra help from all the animals, and her people in restoring their home. She looked over to Prince Omari and an idea formed in her mind. Hoping that Prince Omari would be open to her idea, she headed straight for him. Juliet watched on, smiling, knowing what Iris had in mind. She just hoped that Omari would be lenient with her. Turing back to Amisha, Juliet made sure her saddle was on correctly and not hurting her wings. Then she mounted her alicorn.

"Ready for an adventure?" she asked.

Amisha nodded her head and neighed. Juliet smiled at Amisha's response as she guided Amisha into a trot, to where the others had gathered around Iris and Omari.

"You ready?" Nikolai asked, coming over on his horse.

"Yes," Juliet replied. "Are you?"

"Yes, I'm praying for an easy mission, but I know it will be difficult, nevertheless I still prayed," Nikolai replied.

"I'm sure we'll all be okay, with the God of Light on our side," Juliet said, leaning over to kiss his cheek.

"True," Nikolai said, caressing her cheek as he looked at her. "I'm glad we have each other too."

"Me too," Juliet said, smiling.

As they both rode over to the others, Juliet thought about all that had happened that year. The good and tough times. Juliet hoped she would share more good memories together, with her new family and friends for a long time yet. She quickly said a silent prayer to the God of Light for protection. After, she looked down and saw Nix following beside her whining.

"It's going to be okay," she whispered down to Nix.

Nix continued to follow beside her closely.

Coming up to where Iris, Finnick and Omari were, Juliet was happy that Omari was feeling at ease around them all. Despite being in isolation for years, out of fear for his curse.

"So how does this work?" Omari asked, concerned.

"Well, I'll put my hand on your head once you transform into a griffin, then activate my Gem's power, then I will take on your griffin's appearance," Iris said simply.

"That's it?" Finnick asked. "Sounds easy."

"It took a lot to master the activation of my Gem, and to keep it activated so my animal abilities don't disappear mid battle," Iris explained.

"Right," Finnick said. "Sounds a lot harder, when you put it like that."

"Okay, stand back while I transform, I don't want to hurt any of you," Omari said. The others took a step back.

"You want to try Omari's griffin abilities?" Juliet guessed.

"Oh, you bet," Iris replied, eagerly.

After Omari's transformation was complete, Iris walked over and placed her hand on top of Omari's griffin head. As she concentrated on taking the abilities of the griffin, her Gem began to glow. After a minute, Iris's whole body was covered in feathers. Her feet had transformed into talons, and big brown griffin wings erupted from her back. Opening her eyes, she took in the wonder of her new abilities. "This is so cool."

Juliet smiled at Iris. After losing Jarreth, she was happy to see her friend out of bed and with less puffy and swollen eyes. Iris needed the distraction, and the best way to do that was for her to join the quest. To help her through the grief of losing her father and Jarreth. Iris promised to help in any way she could to defeat the Dark One.

Nikolai rode up to the group with the map in his hand.

"So, in order to reach Mount Solana, we must head north for about two days," he explained. Looking to Omari and Iris he continued. "You should be able to see the mountain before us, so you'll be our eyes in the sky."

"Right," they both nodded.

"Captain Oberon will be leading this mission, so listen up," Nikolai stated, nodding to the captain.

Oberon rode up to the front of the group and took the map that Nikolai offered him.

"Okay everyone listen up, the mission to Mount Solana is only a two day's ride from here. Everybody must stick together, and no wandering off. If you need a break, call out. I will be up front keeping an eye out, and leading the way from the map Princess Iris made us. King Nikolai and Queen Juliet will be behind me, while Finnick covers the rear. Prince Omari and Princess Iris, as King Nikolai said before, you are our eyes and ears in the sky. One flies in front, the other flies towards the back. If you spot anything, let us know."

"Okay," Iris nodded.

"Yes Captain," Omari said.

"Any questions?" Oberon asked the group.

They all shook their heads.

"Good, then let's head out," Oberon ordered, nudging his horse into a walk.

CHAPTER TWO

"The Lord is close to the broken hearted
and saves those who are crushed in spirit."

Psalms 34

As Iris soared through the air testing out her new griffin abilities, she felt at peace, she felt free. These last few days had been tough on her, as she had just lost two important people in her life. However, she did reclaim her home from Jorogumo, with help from the King and Queen of Zolatta. But she needed a break, she needed to be free, and she needed to be away from home as it reminded her of the people she had lost.

Looking down she saw Captain Oberon leading the group on horseback, while looking at the map she had roughly drawn up for him. King Nikolai was riding beside Queen Juliet closely. Iris was a little sad when she saw them close. She knew they were trying not to show affection in public since the recent loss of Jarreth, and she felt guilty for it. Looking towards the back she saw Finnick, looking around and being on guard for any followers of the Dark One, but he also looked lost and sad. Jarreth had told Iris that they were like brothers, and Iris felt Finnick's lost too. At that thought, Finnick looked up and gave Iris a thumbs up, to which Iris did the same, letting him know that the skies were clear.

Her job, along with Prince Omari's, was to inform the others below if they were headed for trouble, or if they found something suspicious enough to report to the captain. They also needed to let them know if they were heading in the right direction to their intended destination.

Mount Solana.

Iris could see the mountain in the distance, and with the pace they were going, she guessed they would have to stop for the night and finish their travel tomorrow. Even though it was originally a two-day ride, Iris hoped to get it done in one, but the horses could only take so much before needing a rest. And she must admit to herself, her arms where the wings covered, were starting to get sore. She looked up towards Omari and saw he was doing well with flying, showing no signs of pain or discomfort. But he had years of flying experience while this was only her fifth. Making the most of her flying experience, Iris went up higher and saw the surrounding area. Since Jorogumo's fall, she had been seeing several types of animals returning to her home kingdom.

Right now, she flew by some medium sized Red Knot birds that were returning to live within the forest that surrounded her kingdom.

"Hello friends," Iris greeted to the lead Red Knot. "Coming back home?"

"Princess Iris, I didn't recognise you. I'm guessing the news of that spider demon is true?" the lead Red Knot asked.

"She's gone," Iris confirmed.

"Thank heavens," the Red Knot squawked. "We could have eaten the smaller spiders, but we had to flee once they got too big, and threatened us and our home."

"I understand," Iris said. "It's great to have you back within our kingdom."

"Thanks Princess," the Red Knot squawked as it started to descend.

Princess Iris was happy that the animals were coming back. Her people had animals as helpers or pets. Each feeling comfortable around the other as there was a special bond between both. All the animals that were coming back would be a significant help when restoring the Kingdom of Kudzu back to its former glory. A whistle sounded throughout the air and Iris looked down to see Oberon waving for her and Omari to come down.

After landing on the soft grass Iris deactivated her Gem, resulting in the loss of the griffin's ability. Omari had landed behind a tree and began the painful transformation back to human. Nikolai went over and handed Omari some clothes as he hid behind a tree.

"Sorry," he called out, embarrassed. "Downside to the transformation."

"Will give you some privacy," Iris called back, then facing Juliet. "Let's get some lunch prepared."

While Omari quickly dressed behind the tree, Juliet and Iris laid out a nice rug for all of them to sit on, and began to lay out some lunch. They had been traveling all day to try and reach their destination quicker, that they had decided to have a late evening lunch. That way they can rest and get up early the following day to continue with their quest. Oberon, Finnick and Nikolai tied up the horses while the ladies prepared lunch. Once the lunch was laid out, Juliet and Iris called the others over, and they all sat down and ate together while their horses rested from the long journey.

"What animal do you like best to transform into?" Juliet asked Iris.

"Oh, that's a tough one," Iris thought for a minute. "A tiger is in my top five, but I love anything with wings. Just the thought of flying and the freedom it brings."

"I can understand that," Omari agreed.

"Why did your father hide you away all these years?" Iris asked.

"He was scared, I guess. Didn't know if I could keep my griffin form under control," Omari answered, as he reached for another sandwich.

"We'll you're doing an amazing job," Juliet told him.

"Thanks," he replied sheepishly. "Nikolai was lucky to have found you."

"I am, aren't I?" Nikolai said, smiling at his wife.

"How did you manage to control the change?" Omari asked Nikolai.

"Whenever I start to feel angry enough to change, I'd find, and or, do something that would calm me down," Nikolai explained. "It was tough at first, but I managed to get the hang of it."

"Find something that calms me," Omari thought out loud, pondering the advice just given.

"What calms you? What hobbies do you like to do?" Finnick asked.

"I like to read," Omari said, in deep thought. "I haven't really had the time to experience much else."

"Reading's a good start," Juliet encouraged.

"Any friends at home that know about your curse? Having someone who knows is always helpful," Nikolai asked.

"Well, there is this one lady. Her name is Kirsten and she's a good friend," Omari said.

"The Captain of the Royal Guard of Neylon?" Oberon asked.

"Yes, have you met her?" Omari asked.

"Briefly, when I was sent as an ambassador to your kingdom,"

Oberon explained. "She is a good solider. You are lucky to have her as a friend."

"She is a good soldier. She's the only person in the kingdom, apart from my parents, who knows of my curse," Omari said, smiling. "She taught me how to fight, and about the world outside of the kingdom."

"Sounds like a good woman," Finnick observed.

Omari smiled and nodded. "I'm very lucky to have her as a friend."

"Friend…. is there more, perhaps?" Finnick hinted.

"More what?" Omari asked confused.

"Stop teasing the lad," Oberon said, playfully hitting the back of Finnick's head.

"Just a friend," Omari assured Finnick.

Juliet smiled and chuckled, then looked over to Iris who had gone quiet.

"Hey," Juliet asked Iris. "You, okay?"

Iris nodded, as she wiped away a tear. "Yes, I will be okay."

"Dottie is amazing, putting all this together for us," Finnick said, taking another bite of the sandwich he held. "It helps as I am on a seafood diet."

"A seafood diet?" Oberon questioned.

"Yeah, I see food and I eat it," Finnick said, grabbing another sandwich.

Oberon sighed and laughed, at least his sense of humour was intact despite the events of the last couple of days. He should make more of an effort to keep Finnick occupied, so he doesn't think too much about the past. There will be a time for mourning later, but right now he needed his lieutenant ready and alert for anything. But Oberon felt for Finnick, as he too missed Jarreth. But he had to stay strong and focused on the mission ahead.

"She is. You know she is our head chief at the palace," Iris told them.

"No, I didn't," Juliet said amazed. "Well, that makes sense. The meals she prepared for us back at camp were amazing."

"Speaking of food," Iris said looking around. "Where's Nix?"

"Probably hunting for food," Juliet replied, taking another sandwich.

"Oh, you don't feed him?" Iris questioned.

Juliet and Nikolai laughed.

"We tried to, but everything we gave him he wouldn't eat. So, we just let him hunt when he's hungry, and he'll find his way back to us once he's done," Nikolai explained.

"That's handy, how did you find each other?" Iris asked, intrigued.

"I saved him in a quest to reclaim my kingdoms weapon, the Sword of the Kings, and now he follows myself or Juliet around," Nikolai explained.

Nix walked up to the group, then went over and laid his head on Juliet lap as she patted his head.

"Good boy, Nix," Juliet said, giving him a good pat.

"Can I pat him?" Iris asked.

"Sure," Nikolai replied.

Iris reached over and was about to pat Nix's head, but stopped when the white wolf lifted his head up and growled at her.

"It's okay Nix," Juliet said. "Iris is a friend."

Nix laid his head back down onto Juliet's lap and whined.

"He's very protective of us. But he's usually good with the people that are around us," Nikolai explained. "Sorry."

"It's okay, I'm still just a new face to him," Iris said. "But he's amazing, a white wolf is quite rare."

"He is. Aren't you?" Nikolai said, patting Nix's head.

"So how far away are we to Mount Solana, Prince Omari?" Oberon asked, looking at the sun descend in the horizon.

"I'd say about half a day or so," Omari estimated. "Give or take."

"Alright, I say we rest for the night as it's getting late and will continue tomorrow morning." Oberon suggested to the group.

"Good call," Nikolai agreed.

"Finnick and I will do a quick scout of the area to make sure we aren't being followed," Oberon said, taking out his broadsword.

"We'll be back soon," Finnick said, following his Captain, axe in hand.

CHAPTER THREE

*"Why did you not obey the LORD? Why did you pounce
on the plunder and do evil in the eyes of the LORD?"*

1 Samuel 15:19

Draykon snuck out of his room when he knew it was safe to do so, being mindful that the staff, guards, and the Lord of the estate were still trying to track him down after his attempted assassination on Lord Blackstone, just hours before. His initial plan had backfired, so he had to improvise.

His original plan was to infiltrate as a mere commoner and work under Lord Blackstone, gaining his trust, then eventually killing him, and taking over his estate. This would give him the army he needed. He would then make his way over to the Kingdom of Zolatta, and take control over the fox spirit he had heard rumours about. He would then bring back his new army to his home across the sea, and take the Kingdom of Keya from its current Queen.

But that plan was ruined the moment he stepped into Lord Blackstone's bedchambers with a knife in hand. It was a trap.

27

Someone had set it for him and instead of Lord Blackstone in the bed, it was one of his guards waiting for him.

Draykon stopped just outside the kitchen, as he heard a noise coming from down the hallway.

"South side has been checked sir," a guard said.

"North side is checked too, sir," another said.

"He hasn't left the estate yet, find him!" the one in charged yelled.

"Yes sir," the guards said running off.

Draykon crept towards the kitchen and opened the door gently and quietly. Once inside he turned around and stood frozen. A group of kitchen staff were huddled together inside, scared.

"If anyone makes a noise," Draykon said, threatening them with his knife.

None said a word, just nodded quickly with tears running down their faces. Draykon walked past them and headed to the other side of the kitchen, where there was a second door that led outside. He quietly opened it an inch and saw two guards running in the opposite direction. Once he did a quick look both ways, he ran out of the back door and straight towards the stables. Hiding behind the stable doors he noticed that there was a lamp glowing inside. Someone was inside. He took out his knife and opened the door, revealing a young boy inside.

"Stay out of my way and you won't get hurt," Draykon warned.

The terrified young boy took a step back and stumbled onto some hay. While the young boy was distracted, Draykon put away his knife and went over and hoisted himself up onto the closest horse. After taking control of the animal, Draykon urged the horse into a full gallop. Bursting from the stables Draykon watched as the guards turned their attention to him and tried to chase after him. But none could match his horse's speed. A few of the men quickly ran to the stables for horses to catch him, but

Draykon was already out of sight.

After riding for a few hours, Draykon decided to stop and rest now that he knew he was safe from his pursuers. He quickly refilled his water flask and looked around at his surroundings. He wondered what to do next as his plan had failed. A stick from the forest behind him broke, and he spun around brandishing his knife. Looking around for the source he saw nothing but trees. After finding nothing Draykon turned back around to fill up his water flask, but took a step back in shock. A women stood before him, smiling at him. Draykon looked around and found she was alone.

"Who are you?" Draykon asked.

"I'm on your side," the women replied.

Draykon looked around suspiciously.

"Don't worry, I'm not with Lord Blackstone," the women said, circling Draykon. "I serve someone much more important than a mere human being."

Draykon eyed her, waiting for her to reveal more information.

"I serve the Dark One," the women revealed.

"The Dark One?" Draykon questioned sceptically.

"The Dark One is powerful, and whoever chooses to follow him, will be given incredible power as well," the women replied, crossing her arms across her chest.

"Power," Draykon thought aloud.

"Yes, he'll give you some, only if you choose to follow and serve him," the women said.

"What makes you think I need your help in obtaining it?" Draykon asked.

The women laughed. "My master has been watching you since you first arrived from across the sea."

Draykon was taken aback. Was it the Dark One who told Lord Blackstone of his motives.

"My master only chooses the best, and he only asks once, so what is it going to be. Power. Or no Power?" the women offered.

Draykon thought about the women's offer. It was tempting. He wanted power as he had lost his chance in getting his own army, thanks to Lord Blackstone. But with power, he did not need an army. After thinking for a moment Draykon smiled wickedly at the women.

"Lead the way," he said.

"Perfect, follow me," the women said, turning towards the forest.

Draykon walked over to his horse and took the reins.

"You won't be needing the horse where we are going," the women assured.

Draykon looked to the horse then at the women.

"If you insist," Draykon said shrugging.

Draykon followed the women as she led him deeper into the forest. The more he followed her, the darker the forest surroundings became. The sun was setting into the evening and Draykon realised by the noise his stomach made, that he had not eaten for a couple of hours. Looking around the forest he tried to look for something that was edible to eat, but nothing stood out. Everything looked old and dead with mould, and no matter how hungry Draykon was, he was not going to eat anything in this forest.

They had been walking for a couple of hours when he had sighed with frustration for what seemed like the hundredth time, and almost tripped over another branch again.

"How can you see where you're going, when it's so dark in here?" Draykon asked looking upwards. "The trees are literally blocking out the sun."

The women turned around and stared at him.

"Woah," Draykon said, almost tripping over.

The women laughed.

"I know my way home, no matter how dark it gets, I'll always know," she said smiling. "Don't worry, were almost there."

Turning back around, Draykon continued to follow the women for another hundred metres. Then finally they both came to a stop just outside of a cave.

"Welcome to your new home," the women greeted, gesturing inside.

Draykon looked at the cave then to the excited women, wondering how he got into this situation.

"Serpentina," a raspy voice called.

"Follow me," Serpentina said taking Draykon's hand.

Together they walked deeper into the cave until they found a lit room. Upon closer inspection, the light proceeded to fill the whole room, and Draykon could see other people waiting and talking amongst themselves.

"Your back Serpentina, and who is this?" the raspy voice asked.

Draykon turned to the source of the sound and stared.

A man sat in the middle of the cave with his hands and feet chained to the wall. His skeletal body made him look malnourished as did his voice. Draykon seem doubtful of the man's power as he did not look the part.

"Come closer, Draykon," the Dark One spoke.

Draykon moved closer and knelt before the Dark One.

"Do you want power?" the Dark One asked calmly.

"Yes," Draykon replied simply.

"Will you serve me as my follower?" the Dark One asked.

"Yes," Draykon replied.

"Welcome to the family," the Dark One said, giving Draykon an apple.

"An apple?" Draykon questioned, taking the fruit.

"Don't you crave power and knowledge. With one bite, you will have both," the Dark One urged.

Draykon looked down at the apple, shrugged, then took a bite. At once he started to feel drowsy and weak, his words slurring as he tried to speak.

"Whaa di you gimme?" Draykon slurred, falling to the floor.

"Power," the Dark One said, smiling above him.

Draykon felt pain shoot up his back and he cried out in agony. The pain then spread throughout his whole body, making him so weak he was unable to move. His body felt heavy as he saw the Dark One looking over at him, while Serpentina stood over his body.

"Do you think he will survive?" Serpentina asked.

"Only if he's strong enough," the Dark One said, closing his eyes.

"You two," Serpintina called out to two of the other followers. "Take him to an empty chamber."

"Yes, Serpentina," they both said, quickly carrying out the task.

Draykon felt his body being lifted by the others, and he opened his eyes slightly to see the Dark One, who was staring right back at him.

"It will be worth it," Draykon heard the Dark One's voice, before passing out.

Chapter Four

*"Do not take revenge, my dear friends,
but leave room for God's wrath, for it is written:
'It is mine to avenge; I will repay,' says the Lord."*

Romans 12:19

Claud stopped and caught his breath as he looked towards the border to the Kingdom of Elaxon. Excitement coursed through him at the thought of his revenge, and he smiled to himself. These past few days of running, gave him plenty of time to think of a few different ways to get his revenge on Issac.

Sneaking behind a stranger's house, he transformed back into his human form and got dressed in some old clothes that hung from the stranger's clothesline, so he could blend in. Once dressed, he walked down into the village to scout his new surroundings, keeping track the number of guards that were present, and scouting out the best route for a quick escape. The guards were all on high alert, stopping anyone who looked the slightest bit suspicious, and checking them out. Claud walked past one of the guards and pretended to accidentally bump into him.

"Watch where you're going, sir," the guard told him.

"Sorry," Claud said, then pretended to have a bad cough.

The guard looked at him with disgust, backing away while covering his mouth with his hand. At least now he was not a suspect.

"Good day." the guard said, before quickly walking off.

Claud smiled at himself in amusement at his acting. He then walked down into the main part of the market and looked around. He walked past some of the fruit stalls and while the owner was busy selling and bargaining with his other customers, Claud quickly stole a few apples, stuck them into his pockets and walked away casually. A few metres down the street he bit into an apple, observing the guards who stood nearby watching over the town's taxman. He knew where he needed to go if he ever needed funds to flee. Walking down a bit further, Claud stopped as he saw the Bellman ready to announce something to the townspeople.

"Attention everyone," the Bellman yelled, while he rung the town bell. "Attention."

The villagers around town who heard the bell stopped what they were doing, and came over to listen to the latest news he had to share. While eating, Claud walked over to see what was going on.

"News from the Queen. If you see any suspicious activities or people, report to one of the guards or the Queen immediately. The Prince of Darkness and his followers are out there, and the Queen cautions you to be careful and stay safe," the Bellman told the villagers.

Claud threw his apple core to the ground and walked away annoyed. Things were going to get more difficult if people were to suspect him. He would have to blend in with the villagers if he were going to find out where the late King was buried. He needed a job, a temporary one. So no one would suspect him while he snooped around the kingdom. He stopped in front of an inn called The Blue Tears. Laughing to himself, he thought it was ironic. The inn was named after the Gem he needed to steal. Walking inside the inn he caught a strong whiff of pork, vegetables, and potatoes. People were laughing and clanking there beers together while listening to the minstrels on stage performing.

"Good evening, sir, how can I help you?" the owner asked, walking up to Claud.

The owner was a bald man in his late thirties with a moustache and goatee. He had a cloth and a glass in his hand, cleaning it as he spoke to Claud.

"I'm looking for work," Claud said with confidence.

"Hmmm," the owner thought. "I have need of a new stable boy but-."

"I will do it," Claud quickly said.

The owner laughed "Okay, the names Bard, what is your name lad?"

"Claud," he replied.

"Claud, follow me," Bard said, heading out back to the stables.

Claud followed Bard out to the stables where he saw another young fellow cleaning out the multiple stalls. The stable hand was a tall and strong looking man. Claud wondered why such a strong looking man was just a simple stable hand.

"James," Bard called.

James turned around and smiled at Bard. "What's up boss?"

"Found your replacement, this is Claud," Bard introduced the two men.

"Nice to meet you," Claud said nodding.

"James is going to become a soldier," Bard explained. "But before you head off, I need you to quickly show Claud how things run around here. Thanks lad."

"You got it, boss," James replied, putting his rake down.

Bard hurried inside after hearing something break and cursed to himself.

"Okay, being a stable hand requires you to look after the horses here. That means grooming, feeding, walking or riding them for exercise, mucking out the stables, putting new bedding down, saddling up the horses when our customers leave, and cleaning their bridle and saddle," James explained.

"Sounds easy enough," Claud replied.

"Yeah it is, but in the busy season the boss always hires an extra hand, as it can become a bit hectic with so many people here," James explained.

"So, when do we take the horses for a ride?" Claud asked, a plan forming.

"Only for exercise and only when all the other chores are done," James reminded him.

"Right," Claud said nodding.

"You like riding?" James asked, giving him a rake.

"Sometimes, but I wanted to visit the Abbey and pay my respects to the late King. Is it open to visitors?" Claud asked, taking the rake from James.

"Sure, the Abby is always open, but you'll have to speak to the current Abbess about seeing the late King," James said, opening one of the stables.

"Thank you, you've been very helpful," Claud said, planning his next move. Claud walked into the first empty stable and started mucking it out, making it ready for the next horse. He thought to himself that his mission might be over sooner than expected. He smiled to himself.

✦ ✦ ✦ ✦ ✦

Issac walked down the hallway leading to the throne room, where

Queen Julia would be hearing the towns people's petitions. He had just received a letter from the Queen's daughter Juliet, and King Nikolai about their current mission, and was hoping he could catch Queen Julia before her next royal duties. Issac was about to open the door to the throne room, when he was interrupted by a servant approaching him.

"Captain Issac," the servant said bowing.

"Ethan, what can I do for you?" Issac asked, turning his attention to the servant. "Priest John is here to see you," Ethan reported, "He's waiting in the library."

"Thank you, Ethan," Issac said.

Issac turned around and headed to the library, wondering to himself what news Priest John had to share. Opening the library door, he walked inside and saw Priest John in a chair reading. Once Priest John saw it was Issac who entered, he took off his glasses, stood up and bowed.

"No need for that Priest John," Issac said, feeling uncomfortable at the formality.

"You will have to get used to it, you are to be King after all," Priest John stated.

"Yes, but that's not until after the war has ended, so the bowing can wait," Issac pointed out.

Priest John laughed to himself. "Of course, Captain."

"What news do you have?" Issac asked. "Is everything okay?"

"Everything's fine," Priest John reassured.

"If this is a casual visit, I'm afraid I am going to have to reschedule. I'm a little busy at the moment," Issac said.

"It's not a casual visit," Priest John said.

Issac stopped and gave Priest John his full attention.

"The Queen has asked me to retrieve something from the Abby for you," Priest John voiced.

"The Abby," Issac said, feeling a little confused.

"Yes, you are to be King soon, so she wanted you to have this," Priest John said, giving him a small box.

Issac took the small box and opened it.

"But-," Issac began.

"Queen's orders not mine. Good day Captain," Priest John said bowing, then left the library.

Issac sighed to himself while staring at the contents of the box. He turned around and walked out of the library and headed straight for the throne room. After knocking on the door, Issac went inside and was grateful to see that Queen Julia had finished with her royal duties for the time being. She looked up and smiled at him, and he could not help but smile back at her. They both walked up to one another meeting halfway, then embraced each other.

"I've missed you," Julia sighed.

"Me too," Issac said, embracing her.

Queen Julia reached up and kissed Issac gently. Issac smiled and kissed her back. "I just met with Priest John," he whispered between kisses.

"And…" she said, knowing what he was going to say.

"Are you sure you want me to have the sapphire Gem?" he asked.

"Positive. As well as the healing ability, it also signifies that your royalty," she said. Issac sighed.

"Hey, are you okay?" Julia asked.

Issac smiled and laughed. "Just a little overwhelmed and not used to it yet."

"Sorry, I did not mean to overwhelm you," Julia whispered.

"It's worth it, just to be with you," Issac replied smiling.

Queen Julia chuckled and kissed Issac again, who did not hesitate to kiss her back.

"Word from your daughter has arrived," Issac said, caressing

Julia's face.

"Is she okay?" Julia asked worriedly.

"She's fine. Just got word that they have defeated the follower who recently took over Kudzu, and they are now continuing with the quest to retrieve the Crystal Gem," Issac explained.

"That's great news," Queen Julia sighed with relief.

"They also said to be careful, as they're not sure if the Prince of Darkness has given up on his pursuit for the sapphire Gem and it's healing properties," Issac warned.

"I wouldn't think so. It's why I have doubled the guards and asked anyone who's seen anything suspicious to come forward," Julia said.

"Good move," he said.

"Thank you," Queen Julia replied smiling.

"And one other thing," Issac said, moving closer to Julia.

"Yes?" she asked.

"I would like to stay by your side at all times. If there is even a slight chance the Prince of Darkness still needs your Gem, I would rather know that you a safe," Issac said, holding Queen Julia's hands.

"If you want to stay by my side always, I think we may have to talk to Priest John," Julia hinted.

"If you're fine with getting married now, then having the celebration later, I'm all ear's," Issac said, then kissed her hand.

Julia blushed then smiled at Issac. "I think we may need to see Priest John after all."

CHAPTER FIVE

"For the wages of sin is death, but the gift of God
is eternal life in Christ Jesus our Lord."

Romans 6:23

The following day Oberon, Finnick, Nikolai and Omari packed up their campsite, while Juliet and Iris went to a nearby stream to fill up the groups water flask, before they continued with their mission. Finnick, who was packing up stuff in his saddle, huffed and sighed while doing the job. Getting annoyed at the small things, he rubbed his tired eyes and continued at a slower pace. Nikolai and Omari, with concerned looks on their faces, were about to walk up and ask Finnick if he was okay but stopped. They saw sympathy in Oberon's eyes as the captain walked over to talk with his lieutenant.

"What are you looking for lad?" Oberon asked.

"I cannot find my copper blade," Finnick said sighing.

"Use mine for now," Oberon said, heading back to his saddle.

After getting his copper blade out, he gave it to Finnick so he could have a quick shave before they departed. As he knew what his Lieutenant was like when it came to beards.

"After you shave maybe we can shear a laugh," Oberon said, trying to crack a joke to ease his lieutenant's mood. After Oberon said the joke, he scratched the back of his head in embarrassment. He was no good at jokes; that was Finnick's job. Always breaking tension amongst the soldiers when needed.

"It's shear madness Captain, you cracked a joke," Finnick replied, smiling half-heartedly.

"Yeah, well don't go expecting no more, that's not me," Oberon laughed with Finnick.

The tension from Finnick was gone, but the sadness and anger from losing his brother was still evident on his face. And that would take time. But at least they could continue this mission without Oberon worrying about Finnick.

We will mourn for him after the Prince of Darkness is defeated, Oberon thought, before turning away to finish packing his own saddle.

After packing up their campsite and organising their supplies, the group mounted their horses and waited for confirmation from Iris that they were not being followed. Iris flew down and landed near Juliet.

"We're all good to go," she told the group.

"Perfect," Oberon said. "As before, Omari is on the lookout from the front and you from the rear."

"Yes sir," Iris said nodding, before flying off to join Omari.

"Let's move out," Oberon ordered the group.

Nikolai and Juliet followed behind Oberon as he led the group towards Mount Solana, while Finnick kept a lookout from the rear. Juliet smiled as she looked up and saw Iris having fun while flying with Omari's griffin abilities. She let out a small yawn as Nix whined while running beside her. Juliet smiled down at Nix then looked at her husband who was staring at her.

"Are you okay?" he asked.

Juliet nodded. "I am. Are you okay?"

"I'm fine, just worried about you," he admitted.

"Why?" Juliet asked with concern. "I'm fine." She then smiled at him.

Nikolai smiled at his wife again. "Your strong, I admire that about you."

Juliet smiled at her husband's praise. She then directed Amisha to walk closer to Nikolai's horse. When Amisha was side by side with Nikolai's horse, Juliet leaned over and kissed his cheek.

"It's because I have you," she said, smiling.

"You give me too much credit," Nikolai said, caressing her cheek.

"I love you," Juliet said.

"I love you too," Nikolai said, smiling at his wife.

Nikolai and Juliet looked up after hearing something above them, only to realise it was just Omari and Iris doing tricks in the air. Juliet looked around at her friends and saw a real connection. Each from diverse backgrounds brought together by the God of Light, to try and defeat a common enemy, and to save the world from darkness. She said a silent pray of thanks for her new friends. After riding for a couple of hours, the group stopped their horses. Oberon whistled for Omari's and Iris's attention to come down. Once they landed and their transformation progress finished, Iris walked over to the group.

"There's too many trees up ahead, so we won't be able to see you," Oberon said. "You'll have to continue on foot."

"That's okay we're not far from our destination," Iris said.

"How far away is the mountain?" Oberon asked.

"Not far," Omari called from the bushes, as he hurried to get dressed. "A couple of miles up ahead."

Oberon nodded and looked ahead.

"Iris," Juliet called. "Hop up and ride with me."

"Thank you," Iris said, mounting Amisha.

"Omari, you can ride with me." Nikolai called out to him. Omari appeared from behind a tree and made his way over to Nikolai.

"Thanks, Your Highness," Omari said embarrassed.

"It's okay, it won't be a long ride. I know you're not a fan," Nikolai said.

The group continued riding for a couple of miles until the trees blocked their path completely. Oberon stopped and turned towards Juliet.

"I think Amisha needs to lead us from here," Oberon suggested. Amisha neighed.

"Oberon is correct, only Amisha knows the way from here," Iris interpreted for the group.

Amisha trotted forward and began to lead the group through the dense forest. After weaving her way throughout the forest, she eventually led the group to a small, secluded clearing. A huge waterfall gushed from the middle of the lake, with beautiful exotic flowers surrounding the lakeside and mountain entrance. But a lake was preventing the group from the alicorn's secret entrance. The entrance stood within view and had vines covering the massive stone doors.

"This is beautiful," Juliet and Iris exclaimed in awe.

"Wow," Nikolai said, speechless for words.

"It certainly takes your breath away," Omari said looking around.

Amisha neighed.

"Amisha said it's called Crystal Lake," Iris interpreted.

"Anyone care for a swim?" Finnick asked, walking towards the lake.

"Uh, I wouldn't if I were you," Iris warned, grabbing Finnick's arm.

"Why?" Finnick questioned.

Amisha walked towards the lake and stopped at the water's edge. Looking in she whined and backed away from the water in fear. Juliet, feeling concerned for Amisha's reaction, walked up beside her, and looked down at what Amisha was looking at.

"Guys, be careful, there's something in the water," Juliet said looking down, trying to find the source of Amisha's uneasiness.

The others came up behind Juliet and looked down into the water. A splash to the side grabbed the group's attention, and they turned towards the sound. But there was nothing there beside a ripple left behind.

Amisha neighed and snorted at Iris.

"What's wrong?" Oberon asked Iris.

"This is the entrance to Mount Solana. The rocks are a bridge to the door, which is found underneath the waterfall. Amisha warns everybody to be careful not to fall into the water as its quite deep," Iris told everyone.

"Across the bridge you'll find a waterfall," Omari recited the riddle.

"Yeah, that's true. Didn't the riddle also say don't look down as it's quite a fall," Finnick said looking at the lake confused.

"Amisha says this lake is different. It's in riddles to protect her kind, so if someone stumbled upon this lake without knowing the riddle, they would get dragged under by the creature that is guarding it," Iris interpreted.

"What creature?" Oberon asked curiously.

Amisha neighed again as Nix came up from behind her and sniffed the lake, then growled as well.

"A kelpie!" Iris said shocked.

"Nix, come here," Nikolai ordered.

Nix growled at the water one last time before walking over

and standing next to Nikolai and Juliet.

"Be careful everyone," Iris warned. "Kelpies are dangerous. They can appear as humans to lure people to them, then they drag their victims under water and drown them."

"Okay, so let me get this straight. We're supposed to cross these rocks to the other side without falling in?" Finnick asked.

"Simple right," Iris said shrugging her shoulders.

"No way, my co-ordination skills are terrible," Finnick said worriedly.

"I'm sure you'll be fine, we just have to cross one at a time and carefully," Juliet said.

Finnick let out a long-frustrated sigh as he watched Amisha walk over the rocks casually.

"What could possible go wrong," Finnick said sarcastically.

After Amisha crossed first without any problems, Juliet followed behind at a much slower pace. Being careful with each step, she eventually got to the other side. Iris crossed carefully like Juliet, being careful where she stepped and how fast she was going. Nix followed behind and stood near Juliet.

"See. Easy," Iris called back.

Omari, after transforming quickly, flew right over the rocks to the other side.

"Cheater," Finnick called out.

Nikolai laughed then followed carefully with Oberon and Finnick behind him.

Swoosh.

A rock flew by and hit the stone door.

"What was that?" Oberon asked looking around.

Swoosh.

"Ouch," Finnick said with his hand to his face.

Swoosh.

Nikolai looked around but couldn't find the source.

Swoosh.

A small rock hit Finnick in the shoulder and he started to slip. He reached out to grab onto something or someone. Oberon caught him just in time, before he fell into the water. Helping Finnick up, the three men looked around for the source of the attack.

"In the trees," Juliet cried out, noticing movement.

Nikolai, Oberon and Finnick turned around and looked at the trees behind them. Seeing movement in one, they reached for their weapons. Emerging from one of the tall trees, a giant anaconda slithered out of its hiding place holding a small rock with its tail.

"Hellooooo boyssssss," she hissed, dragging the words out as she spoke.

"Not you again," Omari said annoyed.

"We meet again, Princeeee," she hissed at Omari.

"Run," Finnick told the others.

Nikolai jumped from rock to rock while dodging the rocks Anna was throwing at them. Once Nikolai was safely across, he turned around and helped Oberon and Finnick cross safely.

"Thankssss, for showing me the way in," Anna laughed. "My master wasn't too pleased when I couldn't find a way in. Now I can get what I came for."

Anna slithered down the tree then made her way across the ground. Once she came up to the start of the bridge, she looked down into the lake and hissed at it, moving back in fear of the kelpie.

"She can't cross, ha," Finnick laughed.

Anna glared at Finnick while thinking, then she began to slither over the first rock. Looking down below she could see the kelpie watching her and waiting for her to make one wrong move. Anna looked back up towards her victims and continued to slither across the rocks carefully.

"You had to open your mouth," Iris commented looking at him, eyebrow raised.

Finnick gulped. "Heh, my bad."

"Quick what's the next part of the riddle?" Oberon asked, taking a defensive position with his sword raised.

Finnick and Nikolai readied their weapons and stood near Oberon, waiting for the anaconda to strike.

"Behind the waterfall is a door of thorns, the only way to remove it, is with a horn," Juliet said reciting the riddle.

"To the waterfall Amisha, we need your horn," Iris said as she ran after Amisha.

Once Juliet and Iris reached the back of waterfall, they both watched as Amisha walked slowly behind it, keeping close to the wall and being careful not to fall into the water below.

"Follow Amisha," Juliet yelled to Iris and Omari over the water's noise.

Both Iris and Omari put their backs against the wall and slowly made their way behind the waterfall, to where Amisha stood waiting for them. Nix began barking at both the kelpie underwater, and Anna, as the snake continued to get closer and closer.

"Nikolai, Oberon, Finnick, Nix," Juliet yelled.

Nikolai turned to see Juliet waving for them to come over. He turned back around and saw the anaconda halfway across the rock bridge. Nix barked at Nikolai before running towards Juliet.

"Come on guys, we can lose it in the waterfall," Nikolai shouted.

Nikolai, Finnick and Oberon ran over to Juliet, who had her back against the wall and was moving carefully behind the waterfall. Nix followed behind her as did Oberon, Finnick and Nikolai. Once they were past the waterfall, they saw that Amisha was already at work on removing the thorns from the stone door with her horn. Once the thorns were removed, the door opened and one by one the group ran inside. Finnick looked back just in time to see Oberon stop with his sword still in his hand.

"Captain, come on," Finnick yelled.

Oberon saw that the anaconda was gaining on them and looked back at Finnick.

"You go on ahead. I'll hold it off," Oberon yelled back.

"Captain, we can make it," Finnick yelled.

"Go on lad, I'll be fine," Oberon said pushing Finnick through the door.

Finnick fell to the ground and looked up just in time to see Oberon smile for the first time in ages, before the door closed locking him outside with the snake. Finnick quickly got up and ran over to the wall and began banging on it.

"CAPTAIN," Finnick yelled, banging onto the stone wall. "CAPTAIN."

CHAPTER SIX

"However, each one of you also must love his wife as he loves himself, and the wife must respect her husband."

Ephesians 5:33

Inside the palace chapel, Queen Julia and Captain Issac stood facing each other while holding each other's hands. The smile never left their faces as they declared their love for one another in front of Priest John, who stood between them reading from the Tanakh. Queen Julia's maid and Priest John's wife stood to Queen Julia's right, as they witnessed the marriage before them. While Captain Issac had Lieutenant Riley and Jonathen, two soldiers who he trained with, and became good friends with, as witnesses to his left.

"I pronounce you husband and wife," Priest John declared, as he closed the Tanakh. "You may kiss the bride."

Issac smiled, then leaned in and kissed Julia, who put her hands around his neck to draw him closer.

"I love you," Queen Julia whispered.

"I love you too," Issac replied, smiling.

"May the God of Light bless both of you, and protect you during these difficult times," Priest John said to them both.

"Thank you Priest John, we will have a proper celebration once this war is over. For now, I just wanted to be close to Julia, to protect her and the kingdoms Gem," Issac told Priest John.

"I completely understand. I look forward to celebrating with you and the whole kingdom in the near future," Priest John replied. "Enjoy the rest of your day, my King, my Queen."

Priest John bowed before leaving the room, as the other witnesses gave their blessings and congratulations before departing as well, giving Julia and Issac some privacy.

"Still not used to being called King," Issac said, looking at the sapphire Gem which was hanging around his neck.

"You'll get used to it," Julia said, smiling at her husband. "Shall we send a letter to Juliet to tell her the news. I'd rather her hear about this from us first and not second hand."

"Of course," Issac replied, taking Julia's hand.

"This gives me a chance to show you our office, and what a royal does during the day," Julia said, taking his hand and walking back to the palace.

As Issac followed Julia throughout the palace and to the office, he smiled at her as he listened to her explain all the things royals must do. It would take him time to learn how to act and what to do at dinner functions, but as long as he was beside her, he was the happiest man on earth.

Issac thought back to his past, as a lonely wanderer, entering the kingdom. When he first saw Queen Julia, he felt sympathy towards her situation and felt a sudden urge to protect her. So, he signed up to be a solider for the kingdom. During his training he had shown exceptional skill with many weapons, and had shown the Captain of the Royal Guard what it meant to work and look after a team. Issac made friends quickly with everyone he met. After a couple of months, Issac was called to an important mission. Issac was relieved to find out that he was to guard the Queen and Princess from others who wanted to harm them. He had never felt this way when helping others, only towards the Queen. He remembered it being a busy few months for him, as Queen Julia and Princess Juliet were attacked, or had an attempted assassination almost daily. But he never gave up, and was always on a constant lookout. After a couple of months, it had quietened down, as people started to become aware of who was guarding the royals. His days of being known as the helping wanderer were over. It felt like he had found his forever home. The days were gone where he would help others in need wherever he went travelling, taking nothing except for a meal and a roof over his head. Now, he settled down in the Kingdom of Elaxon, and found love with the woman of his dreams.

"How does this sound to you?" Julia asked, showing Issac the letter she had written to her daughter.

"Sounds good," Issac said, reading the letter. "How does Juliet feel about us?"

"She's wanted us to be together for years now. She was excited when I told her the news of our marriage," Julia explained.

"Really?" Issac asked, relieved.

Julia turned to face Issac, taking both his hands, and holding them in her own.

"Juliet never knew her father, as she was still so young at the time of his accident. She's told me that she considers you as her father, because you have always been there for her. That's why she wanted you to walk her down the aisle at her wedding," Julia explained.

Issac was speechless. "Really?"

Julia smiled at him and nodded. "She told me herself."

Issac smiled and laughed. "I do consider her as my own child."

"I know. You were so good at looking after her," Queen Julia said.

Issac smiled and looked at Julia lovingly as he caressed her cheek.

"What are you thinking about?" Queen Julia asked.

"The first time I saw you," Issac confessed.

She smiled and blushed.

"Just an ordinary wanderer looking for his next adventure," she said.

"And what an adventure I've had," Issac replied, putting his hand around Julia's waist, pulling her closer.

"And what an adventure we will have together," she said, wrapping her arms around his shoulder.

"As King and Queen, I'm sure we'll have plenty," Issac whispered to her.

"I must warn you, as Queen I can be bossy sometimes," Julia chuckled.

"I can handle that," Issac laughed. "As Queen, what is the first thing you would like me to do?"

"As Queen, I would like to spend the night with my King," she said, smiling.

"I can help with that," Issac replied, smiling as he kissed his Queen.

✦ ✦ ✦ ✦ ✦

Claud finally sat down on a barrel of hay after a hard day's work. He contemplated whether to visit the Abby tonight while everyone was asleep, or leave it for another night as exhaustion was setting in. His thoughts were interrupted by James who came over to sit beside him, handing him a bottle of alcohol.

"The perks of working here," James said, taking a drink.

"Cheers," Claud said, raising his bottle.

"When do you start your training?" Claud asked.

"Tomorrow. I had an introduction last week explaining everything about the role," James said, taking another drink.

Claud watched as James downed his bottle, then offered him his own, hoping the man couldn't take alcohol very well. That way he could ask some questions that James wouldn't normally answer when sober.

"Really, thanks man," James said, a little tipsy.

"Let's call it a favour," Claud said.

James took a drink from the bottle Claud had given him, and laid back on the hay as he stared at the night sky.

"So, who is your Captain?" Claud asked, but knew the answer already. "Good fellow?"

"Don't know, might be Captain Issac, might be someone else," James said, taking another drink.

"Why would it be someone else? Has Captain Issac stepped down as Captain of the Royal Guard," Claud asked, confused.

"No, but rumour has it that he is to be King soon," James said.

"King!" Claud said shocked.

"Yeah, King. He's a very lucky man. Queen Julia is stunning," James slurred.

"What would happen to the sapphire Gem?" Claud asked.

"It will be given to Captain Issac once he becomes King. It's not only a Gem of healing, but it also signifies that he is now royalty," James said, eyeing his now empty bottle.

"Interesting," Claud whispered to himself. "Steal the Gem and get revenge against Issac at the same time."

"Huh, what you say," James slurred.

"Captain Issac is lucky, like you said," Claud expressed.

"Yeah, he is," James said, leaning his head back, and falling asleep instantly.

"Interesting indeed," Claud said, thinking of a strategy.

After a few minutes of James's snoring, Claud kicked his leg to see if he was really passed out. James responded by snoring even louder. Once Claud was satisfied that James wasn't going to wake, he sneaked out of the stables and down the street heading into town. There were people still out celebrating the end of their work week, by drinking and hollering at each other. Claud ignored them and quickly walked past them; his goal was the palace. Once he was close enough to see the palace, he crouched down at the first gate and began counting the guards that were patrolling the area. There were more than usual. If he wanted to get into the palace, he would have to kill a few guards in the process. But that would make things difficult if they managed to raise an alarm before he could get to all of them. He would have to be incredibly quiet, quick, and stealthy. Claud kept low and hid behind nearby bushes and trees as he made his way up to the palace doors. Hiding in the bushes near the entrance to the second gate, he saw two guards at their post, one on either side guarding with their weapons at their belt. Claud snapped a twig between his fingers. One of the guards looked up at the sound.

"The sound came from your side, you check it out," the guard said.

The guard took out his sword and slowly checked the surrounding bushes on his side.

"Closer, closer," Claud whispered.

Once the guard was close enough, Claud took out his dagger and plunged it into the guard's stomach, while covering the guard's mouth to muffle his cry. Once the guard was dead Claud picked up a rock and threw it at the second one.

"Steven," the guard called out. "Steven."

"Slacking off from your duties, are you?" the guard complained, as he walked over to where Claud was hiding.

The guard walked around the bushes looking for his friend. He stopped and called out again. Still no answer.

"Steven," he yelled. "Stop mucking about. Where are you?"

He continued to search further into the bushes for his friend, moving shrubs and checking behind tree's. Claud crept up behind the guard with his dagger and silenced the guard. Once they were both taken care of, Claud opened the palace gates with a satisfactory smile.

"Easy," he said.

Satisfied that there was no one else to stop him, he began his transformation into a wolf. Once complete, he ran through the gate and straight to the palace front steps.

"Hey, get out of here," the guard said to Claud's wolf form.

But Claud did not listen. He jumped up onto one of the guards and bit into his shoulder, then went to the other guard and bit into his leg. Turning around he looked at both of his victims, who lay bleeding quite badly. He slowly walked towards them and attacked them again. As the guards lay passed out on the ground, Claud contemplated weather or not to end them. Thinking it was too much work he left the guards where they were, as they were in no position to call for help and draw others to him. Satisfied that he was all alone and that no one had set off the alarm, he smiled proudly to himself then walked over to the palace front doors. Using his teeth and claws he managed to open the doors, and creep inside. The palace was dark and quiet, but Claud could see well due to his wolf abilities. Walking quietly along the dark hallway Claud sniffed the area trying to find Issac's scent. Once he caught a faint scent of Issac, he followed it. He stopped when he came to a corner, first looking behind him, then down the other hallway, making sure no one was around the palace this late at night. Satisfied that it was deserted, he continued up the stairs to the second level where he continued to follow Issac's scent. The scent was strongest at a door on the second level, and Claud used his claws to open the door. Creeping inside Claud saw two figures lying in bed and let out a low growl.

"For Selina," he growled.

Claud stopped as he heard another low growl coming from next to the bed. He looked closely and realised there was a golden retriever laying in its own little bed near the King and Queens bed. It continued to growl at Claud.

"Issac, I hear something," Julia said, sitting up in bed groggily.

"Is everything okay?" he asked Julia, still half asleep.

Julia looked around the room then stopped and stared at the bedroom door. Fear struck her as she saw a big wolf growling at her only metres away.

"Issac," Julia said in panic.

Issac, hearing the panic in her voice, shot up in bed at his Queens concern. Then looked towards the door where she was pointing. Julia gasped and moved further back in the bed, while Issac reached for his sword that was lying by his bedside table.

"How did it get past the guards?" Julia whispered.

Claud growled again and got ready to pounce.

"Julia, I need you to sound the alarm while I hold off the wolf," Issac said calmly.

Claud did not care that Issac was calling for help, this fight would be over soon and he'll be heading back to his master with the Gem. Claud pounced onto the bed and clawed at Issac, who defended himself using his sword. Queen Julia jumped out of bed and ran through the open door to find help. Issac yelled in pain as Claud clawed at his arm, then he pushed Claud off the bed, where the golden retriever jumped on him and started biting at him. Issac stumbled out of bed and righted himself for the next attack. With his weapon in hand Issac scanned the room and saw the wolf biting the golden retriever, causing it to whine in pain and flee through the open doors. Claud turned his attention back to Issac and lunged for him again. Issac brought down his sword and sliced through Clauds leg. Claud whined but turned around and attacked again. Pouncing on Issac, they both fell to the ground, where Claud tried biting Issac, but Issac held the wolf's teeth away with his sword. Issac pushed the wolf off himself, but Claud managed to swipe at Issac's upper abdominal area with his sharp claws before stumbling to the ground. Issac groaned in pain while clutching his chest and abdomen. Blood ran from his stomach and down towards his leg causing him to feel faint, but Issac stood his ground and waited for the wolf to attack again. Claud, with the sapphire Gem necklace between his teeth, panted for air as he too was dripping with blood. He stood looking at Issac and growled. Issac had managed to injure him. He was about to attack again but stopped as he could hear help coming. The doors burst open with multiple guards coming through to help Issac. Using the distraction, Claud turned towards the balcony, jumped over it, and landed on the grass beneath. He looked back at Issac who stood on the balcony and smiled before disappearing off into the night. He smiled to himself as he held onto the sapphire Gem between his teeth. The master would be pleased with him.

CHAPTER SEVEN

*"But he was pierced for our transgressions, he was crushed for our
iniquities; the punishment that brought us peace was on him,
and by his wounds we are healed."*

Isaiah 53:5

Issac clenched his fist in agony as he lay in bed. Fighting with the
wolf, he had injured is arm, chest, and abdominal area, and Julia
was hurriedly trying to heal him before he lost any more blood.
Before listening to his Queen about staying still in bed, he had
ordered his men to track down the wolf. But as he lay there, he
had heard no word so far of the arrest.

"I'm sorry," Issac said, wincing in pain.

"You have nothing to apologise for. You've done nothing
wrong," Julia said, as she gently caressed his face.

Issac closed his eyes and grimaced. "I lost your kingdom's
Gem, and I only had it for one day. And soon the Prince of
Darkness will have it."

"We can always get a new one. Do not stress, try and relax.
I'm almost done with healing your wounds," Julia said, as she

concentrated. "And your men are trying to track the wolf down, so we may get the Gem back before it gets to the Dark one."

Issac looked to Julia and smiled. "Thank you," he managed to say.

"If it makes you feel any better, I lost mine a couple of days after I received it for my birthday. My mother found it in the kitchen after I snuck in for some snacks," Julia said, now focusing on Issac's chest wounds.

Issac laughed weakly. "That does make me feel a little better."

Issac started to relax as the pain decreased. He guessed that Julia was done with the healing when she stood back and sighed in exhaustion. A maid came up to her and handed her a towel and a tub of water. Julia thanked her as she accepted the towel, and placed the water on the bed side table. After washing and drying her hands she crawled into bed and laid beside Issac.

"Thank you for saving me," Julia whispered.

"Anytime," Issac said, kissing her hand.

"How long do you reckon we can stay like this?" Issac laughed at the thought.

"As long as we like," Julia said smiling up at him.

"What about our royal duties?" he asked.

"Our royal duties can wait a bit longer," Julia said, snuggling closer to Issac.

"I like the sound of that," Issac said, cuddling his wife.

Claud ran as far away from the Kingdom of Elaxon as he could manage with his injury. He had to stop and rest for the night as his injury, which was still bleeding, was getting worse the further he ran on. He found a small cave with a river nearby and decided to stop there for the night. While transforming back to human he dropped the sapphire Gem on the ground. Once the change was complete, he picked up the Gem and looked at it. It was a nice size Gem, but other than that it didn't look like anything special, but then again, he didn't have the power to heal. He hung it around his neck, then went to the river to clean and dress his wounds.

Claud felt pretty good about himself ever since he had stolen the Gem. He had heard about the master's other followers, including Selina his friend, who had tried to steal the Gem before but failed.

Scooping up water from the river, Claud drank a few handfuls and splashed some on his wounds before walking out to bandage them. Holding the cloth in his hands he stopped and listened. There were noises coming from the distance. He could hear multiple men talking and could see lights in the distance coming closer towards him. The soldiers were coming for him. Claud quickly did a quick search and found a tall tree nearby.

"It'll have to do," he said, looking up.

Claud began to climb the tree with difficulty as he had yet to tend to his wound, but that would have to wait. Once he had reached a suitable height, he found a place to sit and got comfortable, making sure he was secure. It was going to be a long night if the King of Elaxon was searching for him. But if the guards from Elaxon were to show up between now and morning, at least he wouldn't be seen from this height. Claud closed his eyes and rested, feeling at peace that his mission was finally complete.

◆ ◆ ◆ ◆ ◆

"*Jarreth, Jarreth,*" Iris cried.

Jarreth woke up gasping for breath. The shock of being in complete darkness made him panic. Sitting up, he looked around at his surroundings and found he was staring at something big, black, and grey to his left. He squinted his eyes hoping it would help him see better, but at once regretted it. Jorogumo lay upside down with a sharp rock impaling her body, her spider legs curling towards her lifeless body. Jarreth backed away, hitting a stone-cold wall, and winced in pain.

How am I still alive? he thought to himself.

Jarreth flexed his body to find that nothing was broken, just a lot of cuts that were bandaged already, and some bruises he had found after moving his body.

How? But his thoughts were interrupted by a noise.

The noise came from his left. He felt in his pockets for his dagger and was relieved to find it still in his possession. After brandishing his dagger, he looked to the left where he heard the noise coming from. Due to the lack of light, he couldn't see anything. After a moment of hesitation, he stood up with his back against the stone-cold wall. Within the darkness he saw a small light floating in the air. The light got bigger and bigger as it began to form into a figure. Not sure what to expect, Jarreth held his dagger out in front of him.

"You can put the weapon away Jarreth, I won't hurt you," said a soft angelic voice.

The figure of light came closer, and Jarreth saw that it was a man. The man was wearing all white clothing, and had enormous white angel wings coming from behind his back. Jarreth stood stunned at the majestic being. He couldn't believe an angel was standing in front of him.

"My name is Malachi and no you're not dead, although you were quite close beforehand my friend," Malachi explained.

Jarreth was about to sign something back, but stopped.

"You can sign to me. I can understand all languages," Malachi reassured. "Even sign language."

Jarreth smiled and nodded, signing to the angel before him.

"*How am I still alive?*" Jarreth asked.

"The God of Light has healed you and your wounds," Malachi began. "You had quite a fall. Broken leg, broken arm, fractured rib, and your head took quite a hit."

"*Why me?*" Jarreth signed. "*I'm nothing but a mute soldier.*"

"You are so much more to the God of Light," Malachi explained. "He has his reasons for the things he does, even though it may seem difficult to understand at the time. In time you will understand why he made you go through your tough situations."

Jarreth thought for a moment before he nodded, understanding what Malachi was saying.

"*So, what now?*" Jarreth asked.

"Go and help your friends. They need you," Malachi said, smiling.

Jarreth smiled and nodded then looked at his surroundings. He looked around for a way out, and found that he could use the rocks to climb out of the pit.

"*Thank you,*" Jarreth signed.

"Don't thank me, thank the God of Light," Malachi said, bowing before disappearing.

"*Thank you, God of Light,*" Jarreth prayed to himself, as he began to climb.

Once Jarreth reached the top of the pit, he took a moment to catch his breath and looked around at his surroundings. The dungeons of Kudzu were in ruins. Dead spiders covered the grounds, and the web's that cocooned people were cut opened and already emptied. Jarreth ran over to the dungeon stair's and was relieved when none of the spiders moved. He climbed the dungeon steps and headed straight out the palace doors into sun and fresh air. His eyes had to adjust to the sun, as he was in darkness for a while, but the fresh air and the sunlight hitting his skin felt good. He was happy to be alive. After relishing the moment in nature, he ran down the palace steps and stopped after reaching the bottom. The kingdom was still in ruins and abandoned.

They must still be at the campsite, Jarreth thought.

He began running in the direction of the temporary camp, remembering the path Lucas had taken him the first time. He was excited to see his good friend Finnick, and his Captain again. They were like family to him. He also couldn't wait to see Princess Iris again, and tell her how much she meant to him.

Jarreth stopped and slowed to a walk once he saw the campsite within view, where the survivors from Kudzu lived for now. Lucas's directions had led him the back way, so after finding the boy's tent, Jarreth peaked inside. Lucas was huddled in the corner of his tent in tears. Jarreth was struck with sympathy for the boy, as Lucas had no one else besides Iris, Finnick and himself. He crawled inside the tent and sat next to Lucas, wrapping his arms around the boy for comfort. Lucas, without looking up, and head buried into his knees, cried harder. He thought it was someone else from the village comforting him. Jarreth sat there in silence while Lucas continued to cry, feeling sad at how his apparent death had caused Lucas so much pain. He wondered how Finnick, Oberon and Iris were coping. Lucas finally looked up, his nose dripping and eyes wet from tears, as Jarreth smiled down at him.

"Your alive!" Lucas sobbed with joy. "How? Everyone thought you were dead."

"*I was close, but the God of Light healed me. Says I'm still needed by my friends,*" Jarreth signed.

"You are," Lucas cried, wiping his eyes.

"*Where are the others?*" Jarreth signed.

"They already left, to continue on with their quest," Lucas said. "I can take you to Queen Athena, and she can give you the details."

Jarreth stood up and followed Lucas as he led him to where Queen Athena was. Jarreth was relieved to find out that Iris's mother had lived, but since Lucas never mentioned her father, he was sad for her loss.

"Queen Athena," Lucas called, from outside Iris's tent.

"You can come in Lucas," Queen Athena replied.

Lucas went inside the tent and Jarreth followed behind him. They both sat down at the seats Queen Athena gestured to them both.

"Who is your friend Lucas?" Queen Athena asked.

"Jarreth. We all thought he was dead when he fell into the pit with Jorogumo, but the God of Light had other plans," Lucas explained happily.

"Oh my, I do remember. I watched the scene unfold while chained up," Queen Athena gasped. "My daughter will be so happy to know that you are alive."

Jarreth smiled and nodded at the Queen, feeling a little embarrassed.

"How did you survive without injuries?" Queen Athena asked.

"I was healed by Malachi, the God of light's messenger. I was told I had broken my leg, arm, fractured a rib and hit my head, but was healed," Jarreth explained.

"Thank the God of Light," Queen Athena praised.

"Can you tell me where my friends are, please, Your Highness?" Jarreth asked.

"The riddle that Amisha gave them, led them to Mount Solana. It's only a two day's ride from here. You're welcome to use one of our horses to catch up with them," Queen Athena explained.

"Yes please, thank you," Jarreth signed, then bowed.

"Lucas could you take Jarreth to the stables and get him some food for the journey?" Queen Athena asked.

"Yes, Your Highness," Lucas replied, standing up.

"*Thank you,*" Jarreth signed to Queen Athena before following Lucas.

CHAPTER EIGHT

"Put on the full armour of God,
so that you can take your stand against the devil's schemes."

Ephesians 6:11

Juliet and Iris stood together, worried about Finnick while they watched him bang onto the stone wall repeatedly that divided them and Captain Oberon. Oberon had decided to stay back and fight the anaconda himself, so that everyone could flee to safety and stop the creature from coming through. He knew the importance of protecting Amisha's kind.

"Can't you open it up Amisha," Finnick cried, begging the alicorn. "Please."

Amisha neighed a response as Nix stood by Nikolai, whining and barking worriedly.

"She can't risk her own race and the Crystal Gem's location. She's sorry," Iris interpreted, with sympathy.

Finnick cried sinking to his knees. He was afraid of the thought of losing someone else. "I know my Captain is strong. But after Jarreth, I-," he tried to explain his reasoning, but couldn't find the words.

Omari and Nikolai both walked over and stood next to Finnick, their hands on his shoulder for support, as the lieutenant continued to worry for his Captain.

"Trust in the God of Light," Nikolai said to Finnick.

"He has his own reasons. Reasons that we do not understand just yet," Omari said sadly.

Amisha lowered her head and snorted, her ears giving away she was upset too. Juliet went over to Amisha and patted her head and whispered to her. "It's okay Amisha, we understand."

Amisha nuzzled her head against Juliet's shoulder in comfort.

"Um, guys," Iris said, looking around at her surroundings. "Look."

Juliet and the others looked over to where Iris was pointing at. A full herd of alicorn's had surrounded the group in concern and curiosity. The head alicorn came up to the group, neighed, then bowed her head. This alicorn had a white and green mane and tail, with a golden horn atop her forehead. She wore a golden headwear and armour around her upper body to signify she was the leader of the herd. Her white and green wings were open showing their beauty and grace. She raised her head and looked to the group. Her ears twitching back and forth with confusion.

"Sorry," Iris apologised, walking quickly towards the head alicorn, and bowing. "We're all just a bit shocked and in awe. My name is Princess Iris from the Kingdom of Kudzu."

"Ah, the young princess who can communicate with different species. A handy gift to have," the head alicorn said, then smiled. "My name is Alvina. I have been waiting for your arrival."

Iris turned around to the others and interpreted what Alvina had said. Then they all bowed and introduced themselves one by one to the leader, still in awestruck at the experience. Alvina smiled at the group then turned to Omari who asked a question.

"How did you know we were coming?"

"The God of Light told her," Iris interpreted.

"Oh, right," Omari said laughing at the obvious.

"Your friend will be fine, young lieutenant. Both of them will," Iris interpreted for Alvina.

"Both of them, I don't get it," Finnick said, feeling confused.

"In time you will, my friend," Iris interpreted. "Follow me."

Alvina turned and walked out of the waterfall. The others followed behind her and gasped in amazement. Behind the waterfall was a whole different world. Beautiful trees grew around the Crystal Lake. There were flowers adorned everywhere, hanging from the cave entrance, to the trees near the lake, and rocks that were embedded in the ground. The alicorn's that lived there looked up and neighed at the new visitors that came into their home. They all had the same colour appearance as Amisha did. White wings, white body, and a golden horn on top of their heads. Their mane and tails all had bits of gold in them, that glistened brightly in the sun. But their mane length, and style were all different. Some wore braids, others curly, and others short. No two alicorn's had the same style, which made them each unique.

"The God of Light is amazing, making no two alicorn's the same," Iris said in wonder.

"He is," Juliet agreed, speechless.

"Look," Omari said, pointing to the nearest alicorn.

They watched the alicorn as it walked up and touched its horn tip against a dying flower. After a few seconds, the flower started to glow and come back to life. Nix excitedly ran up towards the alicorn, stopping in front of the flower. After sniffing the flower he let out a sneeze, shaking his head. The nearby alicorn came up to Nix and sniffed at the white wolf, while Nix introduced himself by licking the alicorn's face.

Juliet smiled at Nix.

"That's amazing how she did that to the flower," Omari exclaimed in wonder.

Alvina neighed again and Iris laughed.

"What?" Omari asked sheepishly.

"The one that healed the flower is a male." Iris told Omari.

"Sorry," Omari said to the alicorn.

The alicorn neighed to Iris. "Honest mistake," she told Omari.

Alvina spoke to Iris as she listened carefully, and after a few minutes Iris turned to the group to share what the leader had told her.

"Each alicorn has their own ability, a gift you could say. It was given to them by the God of Light, to help others in need."

"Wow," Juliet exclaimed, turning to Amisha as she neighed happily.

Alvina smiled at the young alicorn, then spoke again. "Follow me friends, and I will show you what you came here for."

The group followed Alvina as she led them towards the Crystal Lake. Nix ran up and walked beside Alvina, and she nuzzled him before neighing a greeting. The group gasped at the ankle deep, crystal-clear lake before them. Fishes of different kinds swam gracefully below the water as the group continued to follow Alvina to another waterfall. Alvina stopped in front of a waterfall and turned towards the group behind her.

"Behind this waterfall is the door you seek to find the Crystal Gem," Iris interpreted. "I will use my horn to stop the waterfall, until you enter the Cave of Lumina."

"Thank you," Juliet said.

Alvina smiled then lowered her head and activated her horn. The waterfall began to part ways revealing three separate doors. The door to the left was covered in vines, the middle door was covered in chains made of light, and the last door had a carved image of an alicorn on the front.

"The last line to the riddle," Nikolai said, pointing to the door with the carved alicorn.

"Once inside, find a door with fauna," Finnick recited.

Iris walked over to the door with the alicorn carved into it and opened it. Finnick, Nikolai, Omari, Juliet, Nix and Amisha followed behind her.

"Wait, Amisha, Nix," Alvina said. "You must let them complete this alone."

Amisha neighed and stomped her feet, clearly unhappy with the choice, while Nix barked his disapproval.

"They must continue on their own," Alvina pressed.

Amisha and Nix looked to Juliet and Nikolai. Iris quickly interpreted what Alvina had said to Nikolai and Juliet, who then turned to Amisha and Nix.

"It's okay, wait for us here. We'll be back soon," Juliet told Amisha.

"Don't cause any trouble," Nikolai patted Nix. "We'll be back soon."

Amisha lowered her head and snorted, not liking the idea, while Nix barked and whined at Nikolai.

Juliet smiled at her animal's loyalty, then turned back to the door and walked through. Once everyone was inside the door closed shut leaving them in darkness. A few seconds later, the lamps that were inside the cave began to light on their own.

"Okay, that's not creepy at all," Finnick said sarcastically.

"Looks like the light is leading us down this hallway," Iris said as she started walking. "Hey, there's a door at the end."

The group began to walk down the hallway, scanning their surroundings for anything that might lead them to the Gem. But there was nothing but the inside of the cave wall, and the lit-up lamps. Once they reached the door, they saw that there was something written on it. Omari bent down to have a closer look at the inscription, while murmuring to himself.

"What does it say?" Nikolai asked.

"I'm a common household item, I'm found in every single room, I can glow, flicker and shine, I can also dispel darkness and gloom," Omari read aloud.

"Easy, a light," Finnick blurted out.

The rest of the group turned and looked at Finnick surprised.

"What, I read," Finnick said, casually.

Iris raised an eyebrow at him.

"Sometimes," Finnick corrected.

The other's smiled at him.

"Uh guys, something is happening," Omari said, pointing to the door.

The door before them began to open, revealing an exceptionally large room with lights hanging on the wall all around the room. One by one the group went inside, each looking around for another clue. Once they were all inside, the door closed behind them sealing them inside.

"I guess it's too late to turn back now," Finnick joked.

"We'll be fine, we have each other," Nikolai said.

While Juliet, Iris and Omari looked around the room, Nikolai and Finnick took out their weapons, and kept on the lookout for anything threatening.

"Did you guys find anything?" Nikolai called out to them.

"The door we need to go through has a light symbol above it," Omari called back.

"Any ideas?" Nikolai asked.

Omari thought for a second while looking around the room. Once he had done a complete circle of the room he faced the group again.

"Princess Iris, what does the wall to your left say?" Omari asked.

Iris ran over and read the words on the wall. "There's two sets, one at each corner."

"Okay. Princess Iris, Queen Juliet, you both stand towards the left side of the wall, one in each corner," Omari instructed.

They both did as they were instructed, then waited.

"King Nikolai, Finnick, you both stand towards the right side of the wall. One of you at each corner," Omari instructed.

Once they were in position, Omari stood at the main door and turned towards them.

"Okay. This is the Cave of Lumina, and on each corner of the walls there are two tiles. Princess Iris what does yours say?" Omari asked.

"Lumen and dark," she replied.

"Your wall, King Nikolai?" Omari asked.

"Lux and shadow," he replied.

"Queen Juliet, yours?" Omari asked her.

"Lucerna and onyx," she said.

"Finnick, yours?" Omari asked.

"Luce and Tenebrae," he replied.

"Okay, Princess Iris, I need you to press on the lumen tile please," Omari instructed.

Iris turned to the wall and pressed the lumen tile, pushing it into the cave wall. The whole room shook as the main door started opening a couple of centimetres.

"Yes, I was right. We need to press the tablets that mean light in Latin. So, the rest would be lux, lucerna, and luce," Omari explained.

Nikolai, Finnick and Juliet all turned towards their corner, and chose the tile that Omari had instructed. Once they had all pressed the light tile, the main door opened all the way.

Omari turned towards his friends happily. "We did it!"

"Great job Prince Omari," Nikolai praised, sheathing his

sword.

"A job well done," Juliet said smiling.

"Way to go," Finnick said, sheathing his weapon.

"Congrats," Iris said.

Suddenly, the group stopped as they heard a loud grumbling noise. They looked towards each other confused, and were about to run to the door when the floor beneath them suddenly parted, sending them falling into the dark pit below.

"Noooooooooooo," Omari shouted from above.

CHAPTER NINE

"Blessed are the peacemakers,
for they will be called children of God."

Matthew 5:9

"Where are you, puny human?" Anna hissed.

Searching the forest and its surroundings, Anna listened closely to any sound made by the forest or the human. After stopping for a minute and hearing nothing, she hissed her frustration and continued to slither around the trees in search of her prey. She did a full sweep before coming back around to the lake entrance. Anna stood looking at the water and the entrance in frustration. From the corner of her eye, she kept a look out for movement. After a couple of minutes of silence, she let out a frustrated groan.

"You cannot hide forever, human. I will find you," Anna hissed.

Oberon hid behind a big tree to the far edge of the forest, panting with exhaustion with his sword in hand. He could just vaguely see the anaconda at the lake entrance looking for him. But he needed a short break after fighting with this creature. He had been trying to strike the creature to cause some damage, but every time he got close enough to the anaconda, he was at risk of being constricted by its massive snake body. Oberon had to be careful as this anaconda was fast. If he wasn't cautious, the anaconda could bound him with its body, and Oberon would eventually die from suffocation or broken bones. He needed a change in plans, one that would work to his advantage. During his fight he had learnt that this creature was human, but could transform at will into an anaconda. And her name happened to be Anna.

How ironic, Oberon thought, laughing to himself. *Finnick would have loved this.*

Oberon felt terrible when he pushed Finnick through the door, instead of letting him fight with him. But if he was being honest, he felt responsible for Jarreth's death. He was the captain. It was his responsibility to look out for his soldiers. But he had failed, and he felt terrible. He didn't want to lose another good soldier to the Dark One. So, he made the decision to leave Finnick behind.

A stick breaking in the distance brought Oberon out of his thoughts. He listened for movement in the area, and could hear Anna slithering closer to his hideout. Without hesitation he jumped up, sword in hand, and ran back towards the lake. Anna slithered towards her prey with such speed that she caught up to Oberon in no time. Bringing her snake body around, she tripped Oberon. He fell on his back hitting his head, knocking him out for a couple of seconds. He shook his head then opened his eyes, quickly bringing up his sword just in time to protect himself from Anna's fangs striking him. When she striked again, Oberon moved at the last minute so that Anna's fangs caught in the tree root below. Struggling to remove herself, Oberon saw the opportunity to bring his sword down into Anna's body. Anna moved away at the last second and hissed at Oberon before backing away to a safe distance. Oberon ran up again and attacked Anna, slicing her side. Anna screamed and lunged towards Oberon, sinking her teeth into his shoulder. This time Oberon yelled as Anna sunk her teeth in deeper. Dropping his sword, Oberon felt the wetness of blood that dripped down his arm as he began to feel weak. Anna took the opportunity to quickly move her serpentine body around Oberon, tightening her grip. She watched him squirm as she squeezed him tighter and tighter. Oberon tried to stand as still as he could, because if he moved, he would end up dead. Anna laughed to herself, seeing Oberon in distress. Oberon began to feel pain everywhere in his body and wished he could have had a quick death instead of a slow and painful one. Suddenly, he felt free as his body fell to the ground. He coughed and gasped for air repeatedly, grateful to be alive. He rolled over and saw an arrow sticking out of Anna's head. Blood dripped down from her face as her eyes stared back at him, shocked and lifeless. Oberon groaned as he sat up, sighing in relief that another follower of the Prince of Darkness was defeated. That meant one less dangerous person in the world. Well, that's the way he thought about it anyway. Oberon looked up to see a familiar face staring back at him, and laughed to himself.

"Cutting it a bit close there," Oberon said coughing, his hand on his stomach.

"*I could have let it eat you instead,*" Jarreth signed, smiling at his captain.

Oberon laughed along with his second lieutenant.

"I'm glad you're alive Jarreth, the others will be too. You scared us all for a second there," Oberon said, smiling.

"*Sorry it took so long to get here,*" Jarreth signed.

"Don't sweat it, at least your here," Oberon said. "That's all that matters."

Oberon looked over at Anna's lifeless snake body, relieved that Jarreth had made it in time. Jarreth knelt to his Captain and inspected his wounds. Apart from his shoulder wound, there was no blood or open wounds that Jarreth could see. This meant the injury was within, which could potentially be dangerous.

"What is that thing over there?" Oberon pointed weakly to Anna's body.

Jarreth looked to where his captain was pointing to and saw something shining in the sun. Standing up, he walked towards the dead anaconda and saw what his Captain was seeing. A Gem around Anna's neck. Bending down Jarreth cut the Gem free and turned to show it to his Captain.

"*A Gem,*" Jarreth signed, showing Oberon.

"Anna had a Gem on her," Oberon said shocked. "How?"

"*Maybe its hers. People other than royalty can have Gems if they complete a quest or trial. Maybe she obtained it by doing something,*" Jarreth signed, then looked at the light brown Gem.

"Or maybe she just stole it, or stole it from its previous owner," Oberon voiced.

"*That is also a possibility too,*" Jarreth signed, then held it out for Oberon.

"Keep it. You're the one who defeated her," Oberon insisted.

"*You sure?*" Jarreth signed.

"Positive," Oberon said.

Oberon and Jarreth turned around at the noise behind them with curiosity. Amisha neighed at them and moved her head towards the lake while stomping her hoof.

"Help me up, Jarreth," Oberon said.

Jarreth gave his Captain a hand and was worried when he saw his Captain wince. His Captain very rarely got hurt. His opponent must have been strong and fast. When they both looked back at the alicorn, they saw her come out through the waterfall. She looked at both men, neighed again, then turned back towards the waterfall.

"*Do you speak horse?*" Jarreth signed.

Oberon laughed. "No, but I have a feeling Amisha wants us to follow her." Amisha came back out once again and neighed at both men, annoyed.

"Yep, she definitely wants us to follow her," Oberon observed.

✦ ✦ ✦ ✦ ✦

Finnick opened his eyes slowly, as his eyes adjusted to the cave's darkness. He looked around but couldn't see much except rocks, the cave walls and the lamps that hung throughout the cave. Rubbing a sore spot on his head, he sat up and had a proper look around. Remembering what had happened he looked up but couldn't see anything.

"Hello," he yelled into the air.

No reply.

Finnick stood up and picked up his axe, while looking around the room for an exit. He walked over to the cave wall and ran his hand over the rough surface until he came to an opening.

"Bingo," he told himself.

Upon walking through the cave opening, he found himself in another cave room. This room had an underground waterfall. The water from the fall was a light crystal blue colour as it poured out from multiple rocks that were against the wall. Finnick was mesmerized by the beautiful sight. He walked closer to investigate the pond below the waterfall. The pond was crystal clear and Finnick could see fish swimming gracefully below. Hearing movement behind him, Finnick spun around, axe ready, only to find nothing. He walked slowly towards the cave entrance, observing his surroundings carefully. He stopped when he heard a screeching noise to his left. Turning around he saw an unusual creature. This creature was small and brown, with sharp teeth and claws. A small cloth hung around the creature's bottom half of the body, while its upper half was covered in blood and scratches. A tatted necklace hung around its neck showing off many different shapes and sizes of teeth. The small creature screeched as it ran up and attacked Finnick. Finnick manage to get the creature off himself and slammed the creature onto the ground, before bringing his axe down upon it. He looked up at the sound of more incoming screeches, and decided to run while he had the chance. As Finnick ran through the cave blindly, he came across another small creature. This one climbed up onto Finnick's back and started biting and scratching the lieutenant. Another came into view and attacked Finnick from the front. Finnick forcefully backed into the cave wall, injuring the small creature as it dropped to the ground weakly. Finnick now focused on the creature in front of him. A small light came into view and the creature's screeched towards that direction. Once the light was close enough, he saw a man dressed in a robe. A dagger in one hand and a lamp in the other. When the creature lunged at the newcomer, he finished it off with his dagger. Turning towards Finnick the man shouted duck, before he threw his dagger, hitting a creature that was creeping up on the wall from behind Finnick. Standing back up, Finnick looked at the man. He wore a robe with a small rope tied around his midsection. He wore sandals and had a pouch for his dagger. He also wore a small saddle bag that hung around his body.

"Who are you?" Finnick asked, curiously. "And what were those?"

"Simon, Simon peter," the man said, extending his hand to Finnick. "And those, my friend are called screechers."

"Nice to meet you," Finnick said, feeling confused. "Screechers."

Simon smiled then spoke. "Nasty little creatures that attack you, then once your injured enough, they take you back to their lair."

"Right," Finnick said, looking around confused. "Did the alicorn's trap you here as well?"

"No, they did not," Simon laughed. "They are creatures of good. Created by the God of Light to help those in need."

"Then why are you here? Are you some sort of test I need to pass in order to get out of this place?" Finnick asked.

"No. There is no test. I'm here for guidance and support," Simon said, smiling. "And to keep the screechers away from you."

"Guidance and support," Finnick scoffed. "Thanks for the save, but I'm going to find a way out of here, find my friends, then get the hell out of here."

Finnick began walking away from Simon as he began to speak.

"You'll find them when the time is right. For now, let's talk about Jarreth and Oberon," Simon said, sitting down.

Finnick stopped short and gripped his axe tightly. How did this person know of his losses when they have only just met. Finnick turned and looked at Simon, who had already made himself comfortable on the ground. Simon was fishing through his bag until he found two apples and a flask of water, which he set down on the ground.

"Sit down. Let us talk," Simon said.

CHAPTER TEN

"Stretch out your hand to heal and perform signs and wonders
through the name of your holy servant Jesus."

Acts 4:30

"Juliet," a soft angelic voice called out. "Juliet."

Juliet opened her eyes to see a familiar figure on their knees beside her. Juliet sat up and looked around the room, adjusting her eyes to the lack of light in the cave. Juliet turned back and looked at the familiar face, who held a lamp that illuminated the area around them.

"Mildred. It's good to see you. Wait, what happened?" Juliet asked, looking up towards the gap she fell through. "Where are the others?"

"It's good to see you too," Mildred replied. "Don't worry, they're all fine. I'll take you to them soon. I just wanted to have a quick word with you."

"Is everything alright?" Juliet asked, concerned. "Are you okay?"

"I'm happy. I'm living my life for the God of Light," Mildred said, smiling.

"That's great to hear. Are you an angel? What type? Have you seen any of the other angels?" Juliet questioned.

Mildred laughed at all of Julliet's questions.

"Sorry," Juliet said composing herself. "I've just always been curious about all the different kinds of angels that serve our God of Light."

"It's okay," Mildred said smiling. "I'm a normal angel. The one that helps guide people, and pass on any messages from our God of Light. And yes, I have seen the other angels."

"Are they as scary as the Tanakh portrays them?" Juliet questioned.

"Not to me. I've seen them from afar so many times, its normal now. But to others maybe a little. Have you ever wondered why they always say "Do not fear," whenever they approach someone," Mildred said.

"Oh yes, I do remember," Juliet said, remembering a verse from the book.

"Now you know," Mildred said. "How are things for you? How are you going with the earth Gem I gave you? Have you been practicing?"

"Yes, I have. I feel like I'm getting the hang of it. It seems to come naturally to me now," Juliet explained.

"That's wonderful to hear," Mildred said, pleased. "I guess my Gem has come in handy."

"It has been a huge help, thank you again," Juliet said.

"I'm just happy I could pass it on to another who would use it for good and not evil," Mildred said.

"I can understand that" Juliet said.

"There's another thing," Mildred said, with concern. "The Dark One has obtained a new follower. This follower is quite dangerous. He comes from across the sea seeking more power.

You must be careful in the future."

"Do you know who he is?" Juliet asked.

"Only that he is like a dragon who creeps up on its prey. He's cunning and smart and must be stopped." Mildred explained.

"I'll inform the other's and will keep a look out during the war," Juliet said.

"I wish I could tell you more," Mildred said, with concern.

"You have given me information we can use to identify him" Juliet said, reassuring her friend.

"Sorry about the patchy information. The God of Light said it will be helpful in the future. He only reveals what we need to know now. Trust in Him. Everything happens for a reason." Mildred stated.

"Don't be sorry. I'm glad I was given this information. It will definitely help us," Juliet reassured.

"I'm glad I was able to help you once again," Mildred said, standing up.

"I appreciate all you have done, and all the God of Light has done for us. Tell him I said thank you," Juliet said, standing up with Mildred. "I guess this is goodbye."

"Yes, it is, for now," Mildred said, smiling.

"Thank you," Juliet said, hugging Mildred.

"You're welcome," Mildred replied, returning the hug. "Also, to get back to your husband and friends, just follow the lamps that are hanging on the cave walls. If you see any lamps that are turned off, don't go there. It's meant to be a trap for those who managed to get past the alicorn, and have intentions to use the Crystal Gem for evil."

"Right, follow the lights. Thank you," Juliet said.

"See you later," Mildred said, just before she disappeared.

Juliet turned around to the cave's opening, and walked towards the lamps that were on. She was eager to get back to her friends and finish their quest for the Crystal Gem.

✦ ✦ ✦ ✦ ✦

"What do I do?" Omari cried.

Omari, shaking with fear, had his back against the cave wall unable to move. His friends had just fallen through a trap, that opened the floor beneath them. He stood paralysed, trying to think of something he could do. *It's your fault they fell through.*

Omari closed his eyes, trying with all his might, not to let the Prince of Darkness's lies get to him.

"It was a trap," Omari told himself.

Was it?

"Stop it, stop it, stop it," Omari said, hitting the side of his head with his hand. *You're weak, and alone. Nobody cares about you.*

Omari tried his hardest not to let the words get to him. But right now, he was alone and weak. He had no way to find his friends and didn't know what else to do. Omari looked towards the exit.

"*I can't find them while standing here*," Omari said to himself. He wiped his eyes then readied his gauntlets and walked through the door. Once he was on the other side, the door shut behind him. Omari jumped back at the sudden noise and was still for a minute, praying there were no more traps.

Omari sighed a relief.

Turning around he continued down the hallway, following the lamps that hung on the cave walls. Then he came to a fork in the road. One corridor had lamps lighting the way, the other had none and was full of darkness.

"That would be a big nope to the darkness," Omari told himself, as he walked down the lit corridor.

Omari jumped at the noise of fallen rocks coming from behind him. He turned around to find the culprit, but there was no one there. Clenching his fist, he continued on.

"The God of Light is with me, the God of Light is with me," Omari kept telling himself repeatedly.

Another noise sounded behind him, and Omari jumped around with his fist raised. But saw nothing.

"Nikolai," Omari called. "Finnick."

No answer.

"Do not fear. Do not fear," Omari kept reciting the words from the Tanakh.

He turned back around and continued walking down the hallway, but this time he increased his speed. From behind, he could now hear clattering and screeching noises, and they were coming fast. Turning around to face them, he held his fist up ready for a fight.

"Hello," Omari called out.

Omari stood his ground and waited. Out of the darkness jumped a small creature. It was tiny, but then Omari saw its sharp claws and teeth as it screeched at him. The creature jumped up onto Omari and started scratching at his face. Omari reached for the creature and smashed it forcefully to the ground with his Gem's strength. He stood there and waited for the creature to get up but it didn't. From a distance he heard more screeching noises coming his way.

"Yeah nope," Omari said, turning around to run.

Out of the darkness a creature jumped up at him and attempted to claw at Omari's face. Omari blocked himself, and after taking hold of the creature, threw it onto the ground. The creature jumped back up and began to attack again. This time Omari punched it hard, and it slammed into the cave wall and slumped to the ground.

"Gosh its fast," Omari said shocked, looking around.

He saw the one that had attacked him first, then the second.

"There's more than one," he told himself with dread.

Omari turned around and began to run down the cave hallways, being mindful to stay in the lit-up areas. He could hear screeching and clattering noises in the distance but didn't stop, he just kept running. After running for a couple of minutes, Omari slowed down as the creature and the screeching noises were finally gone. He looked back to where he came from, as he walked slowly and sighed, he was safe again. Turning to face the front, he began to walk, but the floor gave way to nothing. Omari fell through the hidden trap within the shadows. He reached around for anything he could hold onto and found a rock protruding from the wall. Looking down he realised that he was dangling from a cliff within the cave.

"Damn," Omari huffed.

Then Omari could hear the sound of footsteps, as they became faster and louder. Omari wasn't sure if it was a friend or foe, but his hands were getting sore, and the cliff looked deep. He needed help.

"Hello," a soft voice called out.

"Hello," Omari yelled.

"Where are you?" the voice asked.

"Dangling from the cliff," Omari answered.

"Oh, I guess the alicorn's have outdone themselves to protect this place," the voice said. "Hang on I'm coming."

Omari looked around for the source of the voice. Then a young man with curly black hair, dressed in fine robes, and a book in his hand came into Omari's view.

"Oh, there you are," the young man said with a smile.

The young man put his book down, got down onto his knees and gave Omari his hand for support. Omari grabbed the stranger's hand and was lifted away from the edge. Both men sat on the floor, resting from the sudden event.

"Thank you," Omari said, nodding to the young man. "I'm Omari."

"I'm Matthew, and you're very welcome," Matthew said, reaching for his book and holding it close to his chest "Are you okay?"

"Yeah, I'm fine. Just lost my footing," Omari said sheepishly.

"Don't worry, we all get lost at one point in our lives. Some more than others," Matthew said, standing up. "Let me show you the way out."

"Thanks," Omari said, taking Matthews offered hand. "But I need to find my friends first, then the Gem."

"The Crystal Gem," Matthew enquired.

"Uh, how did you…" Omari began.

"I can show you the way," Matthew said.

"You know where the Crystal Gem is hidden?" Omari asked, shocked.

"Yes," Matthew said. "Follow me."

Omari stood staring at Matthew, shocked, not sure whether he was a friend or foe. He certainly didn't dress like an evil person. But you can't judge a book by its cover, and Omari had to know.

"What is the matter?" Matthew asked, stopping, and turning towards Omari.

"Why are you down here?" Omari asked.

"To help and guide you to your friends and the Gem," Matthew said nonchalantly.

"Are you trapped here too?" Omari asked.

"Nope, I was sent down here," Matthew said, turning back around and continuing down the cave hallway.

"Sent by whom?" Omari asked, following him.

"The God of Light," Matthew said, casually.

Omari relaxed and continued to follow Matthew. He seemed to know the way through this maze, and was willing to take him straight to his friends and then the Gem. A noise distracted Omari from his thinking, and he turned around to find the source.

"Be sure to keep up," Matthew called. "Don't stray anywhere that has no light."

"Why not?" Omari questioned.

"We're not the only ones in here, there are others down here. I call them screechers. They attack the lost and bring them to their master who is trapped further down below. Deep in the cave, the God of Light trapped a beast and created the alicorn race to protect the cave from outsiders. They keep the beast trapped below to protect humanity." Matthew explained.

"Wow. So that's what the noise was," Omari said with dread. "A screecher."

"It was trying to injure you enough to take you back to its master," Matthew said, taking a turn to the left.

"It's master." Omari inquired.

Matthew stopped and turned towards Omari. He held his book close to his chest as he tried to find the right words.

"The beast that is trapped down here is the Leviathan," Matthew said, shivering at the mention of the name.

"You mean the one from the Tanakh. The one that only the God of Light can defeat," Omari said with unease.

"Yes," Matthew replied.

Omari swallowed the lump in his throat and continued to follow Matthew, making sure he could still see the man that was so generously helping him. But Omari couldn't stop thinking about the beast trapped below. He prayed that his friends were okay, and hoped he would see them soon.

CHAPTER ELEVEN

"Look at the birds of the air; they do not sow or reap or store away in barns, and yet your heavenly Father feeds them."

Matthew 6:26

"How do you know about them?" Finnick asked, turning around to face Simon.

"I was told by my teacher," Simon said, casually.

Finnick blinked away the tears that were forming in his eyes and rubbed them, suddenly feeling very tired and drained.

"Your teacher, what are you, a student?" Finnick asked.

"Of a sort," Simon replied, offering Finnick some cut up apples.

Finnick took some and sat down with Simon. They ate in silence as Finnick relished the food, grateful to be eating as he was starving. Then he thought about his friends and frowned, putting the apple on the ground. He shouldn't be eating at a time like this, not when his friends could be in trouble.

"What troubles you?" Simon asked.

Finnick looked to Simon and hesitated for a moment. Realising

Simon was a patient person, in defeat he began to open up.

"I lost my friend who I consider a brother," Finnick confessed.

"Jarreth," Simon said.

"Yes. He was killed by the Prince of Darkness's second in charge, Jorogumo," Finnick explained. "Also, my Captain, who is like a father to me, took on one of the Dark One's followers, and wouldn't let me assist him. What if…?"

"Ah yes. Captain Oberon," Simon said. "He is known throughout the kingdoms as a very good and honest Captain."

"He was, I mean he is. I have to think positive," Finnick told himself.

"Can I speak freely?" Simon asked.

"Of course," Finnick replied.

"When I lost my friend and teacher, I was a wreak. He was innocent and yet they killed him," Simon said, clearing his throat.

"I'm sorry," Finnick whispered, knowing the pain he had, mirrored his own. "How did you cope?"

"I started telling people all the good things he had done for others, while he was alive," Simon said, smiling. "He changed so many people's lives, helped those that others wouldn't help, and did amazing things," Simon said, smiling at the memory.

"You didn't seek revenge on the ones who killed him?" Finnick asked.

"No. My friend wouldn't have wanted that," Simon replied, smiling. "He would have wanted me to help other's the way he did. And I did that."

"So, no getting revenge," Finnick said, nodding at the hint Simon was giving him.

"It's up to you, but I would advise against it," Simon said, patting Finnick on the back.

"Thank you," Finnick said. "For listening."

"No problem," Simon said standing up.

Finnick stood up after Simon and followed him as he led them both through the cave.

"Come, I'll show you where your friends are," Simon said.

"You know where they are?" Finnick asked.

"No," Simon said smiling. "But I know where they will end up."

"End up," Finnick said confused. "Now you're talking in riddles."

Simon laughed as he patted Finnick on the back.

"There's only one way out of this cave, so I will take you to where your friends should be, if they have found their way through," Simon explained.

"They will be there," Finnick said, having faith in his friends.

"They will," Simon agreed.

Iris woke up and looked around, trying to adjust her eyes to the darkness of the cave. Looking up she tried to see where she had fallen from. Unfortunately, all she saw was darkness. Standing up she stretched out her sore limbs but stopped as her arm gave her terrible pain.

"Ouch," she said, observing her arm.

She stretched out her right arm and tried to move her fingers slowly, wincing in pain as the joints moved. Taking out a small torch from her pocket, she looked around and tried to find something that would act as a splint just in case it was broken. Hopefully, she could find Juliet soon so she could mend it, but the maze looked like a labyrinth. She heard some rocks fall from behind her and spun around to see what was there. To her surprise, nothing.

"Huh, weird," Iris said.

The fallen rock sound had come from another cave opening, which had lights hanging on the wall. She decided that's the way she would go, and she'll try to find a stick for her arm on the way. The longer she stayed in one place the more uneasy she felt. She had to find her friends. Walking over to the lit cave opening she stopped and listened, as she heard someone calling her name.

"Iris," the voice called, sounding distance.

Iris followed the voice to another cave opening that was full of darkness and tried to listen further.

"Anyone there?" the voice called again.

"My friends," Iris said happily, about to walk towards the voice.

"STOP," Iris heard a voice.

"What makes you think a human can understand us. There's no point trying every time, hon," said another voice.

Iris stopped and turned, trying to find the voice that she was hearing much clearer and closer now.

"Look she's turning around, that means she can hear us," the voice said excitedly.

"Yeah, with your yapping, everyone can hear you," another voice said.

"I cannot have another taken away and eaten on my conscience," yapped the voice.

"Who's there?" Iris called out.

"You can understand us, love," the voice said shocked.

Iris smiled then spoke. "My name is Iris. I'm the Princess from the Kingdom of Kudzu. The Gem which was given as a gift to the royals of my kingdom, was the amethyst Gem, which allows me to talk to animals."

"Oh, how wonderful, someone who can understand us," the voice said.

"Yes, finally someone else who can listen to you, besides me," said the other in relief.

"Where are you? What are you?" Iris said, turning around and looking everywhere.

"Down here love, my name is Sally," the voice said below. "This here is Sam. And we're both salamanders."

Iris smiled as she bent down towards the ground meeting the two salamander's who sat on a rock, near the entrance that was surrounded with darkness. They were small and orange with black spots covering their body.

"Hello," Iris greeted, sitting on the ground near them.

"Hello Princess, it's nice to meet royalty," Sally said, happily.

"It's nice to meet anyone down here," Sam said, unamused.

"Excuse Sam, we don't get a lot of visitors to this cave," Sally said, hushing Sam with a look. "What brings you to the Cave of Lumina?"

"There's a powerful evil about, and to defeat him we require the Crystal Gem. My friends and I are here to find it," Iris explained.

"Oh my, well you've come to the right place. Let us show you where it is, and maybe we'll meet your friends along the way," Sally said, hopping off the rock.

"Unless they've been eaten," Sam said, following Sally onto the ground.

Sally gave Sam another look as they both stood ready at the cave that was lit up with lights.

"Eaten," Iris said with disgust.

Sally sighed and turned towards Iris. "The Crystal Gem isn't the only thing the alicorn's are keeping safe."

"Okay, what else are they hiding?" Iris said, almost too scared to ask.

"Hiding! More like keeping it in to protect mankind from chaos," Sam said.

"Okay," Iris said slowly. "What are they keeping in this cave, to protect us from?"

"The Leviathan, a nasty beast. The Leviathan is the embodiment of chaos and death. Only the God of Light has authority over it. He is also the only one who can kill the beast," Sally explained.

"Okay," Iris said, trying to control her breathing as she processed the news.

"Great," Sam said with dull tone. "You scared her."

"Oh my, sorry dear," Sally said worriedly.

"I'm okay. I'm more concerned about what Sam said about being eaten, and where my friends are," Iris said, taking a breath.

"In the past when alicorn's and humans lived in peace, someone came into the Cave of Lumina and tried to free the beast. After that the God of Light sealed it deeper within this cave and had the alicorn's guard it to protect mankind," Sally said.

"So, its trapped. I don't understand what Sam means by 'eaten'," Iris said.

"Screechers, nasty little things. They are small and brown-," Sally began.

"And ugly," Sam chimed in.

"They have sharp teeth and claws, and they bring lost victims to the leviathan since it's trapped," Sally said.

"How many people come down here?" Iris asked confused.

"Years ago, when the leviathan was put in here, alicorn's went into hiding in fear of being used to get access to the cave. Eventually the God of Light created a sanctuary for them near the Cave of Lumina, to protect them and others. But before that, many people used to come to try and find the Crystal Gem for power. When they got lost, they would eventually be taken by the screechers," Sally said.

Iris shivered at the thought, hoping, and praying to the God of Light that her friends were okay.

"Wait," Iris said. "Is that why you stopped me from going into the dark part of the cave?" Iris asked.

"Yes, the screechers can mimic sound. That voice you thought was your friends, wasn't. It was a screecher trying to lure you in," Sally said.

"Oh," Iris said terrified at the thought. "Thank you."

"You're welcome love. Now, let's find those friends of yours," Sally said, leading the way.

Iris prayed once more to the God of Light before following Sally and Sam, thanking Him for the salamanders, and the lights guiding them through the cave.

CHAPTER TWELVE

"Have I not commanded you? Be strong and courageous.
Do not be afraid; do not be discouraged,
for the Lord your God will be with you wherever you go."

Joshua 1:8

Nikolai woke up by the sound of a low growl nearby. Sitting up quickly, he looked around the cave trying to find the source.

"Ouch," Nikolai observed, rubbing his head.

The last thing he remembered was solving the riddle with his friends then falling. Looking around the room he could see nothing but darkness; reaching out he tried to feel for where his sword was. After fumbling around in the darkness, his hands finally found the coldness of the blade. Relief flooded through him. Reaching for his fallen sword he activated his topaz gem, which engulfed into flames and lit up the entre room. He guessed he had fallen into another part of the cave, as did the others, as he could not see anyone else. He stood up slowly, checking to see if he had any unknown injuries, but also to see what dangers were in the room with him. Looking around he stared in amazement at the lake a few metres away from him. A movement in the water to his left caught his attention and he turned to observe. Seeing a black shadow move swiftly through the water, Nikolai backed away. The water was a nice clear blue, so clear that Nikolai could see the monstrous creature swimming below. Moving back towards the safety of the rocks and cave walls, he turned to find some sort of ledge so he could climb out. But from where he stood there was nothing, he was trapped. Hearing something exit the water, Nikolai turned to find the creature crawling out from the depths below. The leviathan stopped mid-way watching Nikolai, its sharp claws holding onto the rocks to support its weight. It growled at Nikolai showing its many teeth.

"Don't panic, don't panic," Nikolai told himself.

"Don't panic," the creature mimicked, in a monstrous voice.

Nikolai stared at the creature in shock as it repeated what he had said moments earlier. Fear struck him.

What kind of creature is this? Why is it in the Cave of Lumina? Maybe the alicorn's are guarding it; to prevent it from escaping, he thought.

He would have to ask them if he got out.

When I get out, Nikolai thought.

The creature moved forward and revealed more of its scaly body which hid beneath the water. Nikolai took a step back and remembered he was touching the cave wall. Looking out of the corner of his eye, he tried to find a way out while keeping eye contact with the creature. This creature was a textbook leviathan. The scales that covered its body looked impenetrable. Its jaw glowed orange as smoke came trailing out, meaning the creature could breathe fire. According to the Tanakh, the leviathan was a serpent who lived in the depths of the ocean. It made sense, it had to be the leviathan. From the corner of his eye Nikolai saw shadows moving along the upper part of the rocks. He moved an inch but stopped when the creature moved with him. He stared at the leviathan who was almost out of the water, its long scaly tail still submerged.

"Don't panic," the creature mimicked again.

"God of Light, help me," Nikolai whispered.

"God of Light," the creature mimicked with a grotesque sound. "God of Light."

Nikolai didn't know what to do, he was trapped. He looked around again at the cave room trying to find somewhere he could go, but the only way out was up. Turning back around to the leviathan, Nikolai stumbled, shocked at how close the creature had gotten while he was distracted.

"This can't be the end," Nikolai cried out, as the creature got closer and closer. Nikolai closed his eyes and said a small prayer for Juliet and his friends.

"Heads up," Nikolai heard a familiar voice yell.

Nikolai looked up to see Omari with another person. They were both standing higher up on the rocks within the cave.

"Wow you fell pretty far down," Omari said, with concern.

"We need to get him out quickly, nobody is supposed to be down there," Matthew said, agitated. "It's home to the leviathan, and only the God of Light can tame and defeat it."

"On it," Omari said without hesitation.

Nikolai watched as Omari tried to find something he could use to get down and back up again. But there was nothing around.

"Don't panic," Nikolai said, turning towards the sound of the creature. "God of Light, help me."

"Oh man," Omari said in shock, as he finally saw the creature below.

"Oh man. Oh man," the creature copied.

"Somebody do something," Nikolai called out.

"I- um- I don't know what," Matthew said looking around

confused. "I'm not a fighter."

"Good thing I am," Finnick yelled coming into view, with Simon behind him.

"What's wrong? How did you get down there?" Simon yelled down.

"I fell," Nikolai called back. "It wasn't by choice."

"Does anybody have any rope?" Simon asked, looking around at the others.

"We didn't come prepared," Omari said sheepishly.

Hearing the grotesque noise in front of him, Nikolai moved out of the way from the incoming leviathan that lunged towards him. He almost missed it, but the leviathan was too quick. Sinking its teeth into his arm, Nikolai cried out. He brought his sword up with his other hand, and activated it, creating a wall of fire between him and the creature, hoping it would keep it away. The leviathan backed away and let out a monstrous roar, its eyes on Nikolai and his flaming sword. Nikolai collapsed onto the ground while looking at the creature staring back at him.

"Yes, you injured it," Omari praised.

"No," Matthew said, sharing a concerned look with Simon. "This leviathan can only be tamed and killed by the God of Light. No one else."

The leviathan walked back and forth, assessing the best way to attack. Nikolai held onto his sword tightly as he tried to stay focused, but his vision was getting blurry as the blood trickled out of his wound. The leviathan roared once more before getting ready to attack its prey once more. Then it pounced at Nikolai who closed his eyes waiting for the inevitable.

"Noooo," Omari and Finnick yelled from above.

With his eyes closed Nikolai felt something wrap around his mid-section. He opened his eyes and saw that it was vines that were pulling him up towards the others. Looking back down at the leviathan, Nikolai saw it smash headfirst into the rocks where Nikolai stood only moments earlier. It looked up at Nikolai and let out another roar at its fleeing victim. Once Nikolai was safely on the ground with the others, Juliet ran up to him and hugged him tightly.

"I'm sorry I'm late," she cried.

"Better late than never," Nikolai said smiling.

"Iris," Omari exclaimed, overjoyed to see Iris entering the room. "We're all back together."

"Is everyone okay?" Iris asked looking around.

"Everyone except for the King," Finnick pointed out.

Ending the embrace Juliet looked at his wounded arm, then around at the others.

"Who else is hurt?" she asked.

Iris was the only other to raise her hand.

"But King Nikolai's wound needs urgent attention, mine can wait," Iris reassured.

Juliet nodded then turned and started healing Nikolia's arm.

"I knew the God of Light created the Gems, but seeing them being used is another thing entirely," Simon said amazed.

"Yes, it is quite a sight," Matthew said writing in his book.

"How did you all find your way through the caves?" Nikolai asked, wincing as he moved to see everybody.

"Simon helped me," Finnick said pointing to the man.

"Hey," Simon greeted.

"Matthew helped me," Omari said, pointing to the man writing in his book.

"I'm happy to meet everyone," Matthew said smiling.

"Me, I had help from Sam and Sally. They're cave salamanders," Iris said pointing towards the ground at the two amphibians that stood by her side.

"Magnificent," Matthew said aloud. "The amethyst Gem that

allows a person to communicate with animals."

"Yup, it's pretty awesome," Iris laughed.

Juliet smiled as she continued to heal Nikolai. With the wound almost healed she was happy there was no immediate threat to her family and friends.

"I'm sorry everyone," Omari confessed aloud.

"Sorry for what?" Nikolai asked, moving his now healed arm around to check it.

"The floor giving way-," Omari began.

"Wasn't your fault," Iris said.

"Iris is right," Juliet said, as she beckoned Iris to come over.

"We couldn't have known the floor was going to open up, and besides we're all fine," Finnick said, side hugging Omari.

"Your arm is just dislocated, I'm going put it back in then heal the rest," Juliet explained as she began.

Iris let out a grunt as Juliet put her arm back into place.

"I'm good, I'm good," Iris told herself.

Nikolai looked back down at the leviathan and shivered when he realised it hadn't left, and was just staring up at them patiently.

"I've never seen anything like it," Finnick said.

"I've read about it, but never thought I would see one in person," Omari said.

The leviathan growled at the group that was watching it.

"At least you dealt with the screechers," Simon told them. "And not the leviathan itself."

"Yeah, that's true" Finnick agreed.

"What are screechers?" Juliet asked.

"The screechers are small devilish creatures who trick anyone and anything into going down there," Simon pointed to the leviathan. "To feed it."

"Oh," Omari said, starting to panic.

"Alright," Juliet said standing up with Iris. "Let's get out of here."

"Follow me," Iris said scooping up the two salamanders into her hand.

The others followed behind Iris as Sally and Sam told her which way to go. They were glad for the two guides, as the cave had many twists and turns they had to take, as they were quite far from their original path. They all hoped they would get to the Crystal Gem soon, and out of the cave with its secrets and riddles.

CHAPTER THIRTEEN

*"He brought them out of darkness, the utter darkness,
and broke away their chains."*

Psalms 107:14

"Here it is," Sally told everyone.

The group walked into another room within the cave, but this one was different from the others. This room held the Crystal Gem. It floated in the middle of the room on a pedestal, which lit up the whole room. Iris put the salamanders on the ground and thanked them one last time before they scurried off back to their home.

"Wow," Finnick said, circling the Gem.

"It's amazing," Omari exclaimed, inspecting it.

"It's a gift from the God of Light, to aid the one who fights against the Prince of Darkness," Matthew told the group.

"It will certainly help in the upcoming war against him," Nikolai said, sharing a smile with his wife.

"I cannot believe we found it," Juliet said in awe.

Iris stared at the Gem with tears in her eyes, wishing her father and Jarreth could see their small victory against the Dark One. She wiped the tears away and said a silent prayer of thanks to the God of Light.

"Iris," Juliet put a hand on her shoulder. "Are you okay?"

Iris nodded while wiping her eyes. "Just wish my father and Jarreth could see this."

"And the Captain," Finnick said as well.

"And the Captain," Iris added.

Simon put a comforting hand on Finnick's shoulder as Omari and Matthew went up towards the Gem to inspect it.

"It's a bit big to fit inside the King's sword," Omari observed.

"The power that is radiating from the Gem is quite strong," Matthew noted, as he wrote notes into his book.

"Before anyone touches the Gem, please make sure this room doesn't hold anymore traps?" Nikolai asked everyone.

Each person walked around the room trying to find any source of a quest, trap, or riddle. When they finished, they met back in front of the Gem.

"Nothing as far as I can see," Omari said.

"Same here," Finnick agreed.

Nikolai looked to Juliet. "Anything?"

"No," she shook her head.

"There seems to be some sort of riddle written on the pedestal," Matthew said inspecting it.

"I'm beginning to dislike riddles," Finnick said frustrated.

"You and me both," Simon said crossing his arms. "What does it say Matthew?"

"It says,

The one who takes the bling.

Must be crowned a king.

The one who is not.

Will most surely rot." Matthew read out loud.

"What does that mean?" Finnick asked. "Will you really rot if you're not worthy?"

With her eyebrows raised, Iris pointed to the side of the room showing a human skeleton lying to the side clutching their arm.

"Point taken," Finnick said, then turned to his King. "You ready King Nikolai?"

Nikolai hesitated at the sight of the skeleton, then turned to face the pedestal. He walked up towards the Gem, stopping when he was in front of it. Looking at the Gem he said a silent prayer for safety, then reached out and took a hold of the Gem. The Gem began to glow brighter as Nikolai held it in his hand.

"Wow," the group said in awe, as Nikolai turned to face the group.

Suddenly, the whole cave lit up with a bright white light. The group had to look away and shield their eyes as the Gem shone brighter within the cave. Once the light faded, the group turned and stared at the being that stood behind Nikolai.

"Welcome friends," a soft angelic voice said.

"Mildred!" Nikolai said, both shocked and happy to see an old friend.

"Who?" Finnick asked.

"Mildred turned away from the Prince of Darkness, and sacrificed her life to save Juliet's during the attack on our kingdom," Nikolai explained to the group.

"How are you here?" Finnick asked.

"I'm here to protect the Crystal Gem and it's powers, and to make sure that the user doesn't use it for evil," Mildred explained. "But it seems I don't need to worry about who's taking it. You figured out the cave and the riddle, congratulations."

"We did it with the help of Princess Iris and her Gem's abilities," Omari said.

"We did it as a team," Iris said.

"Well done," Mildred said. "The road ahead will be tricky and dangerous but together you will make it through, I have no doubt. Good luck in your travels and may the God of Light bless you in your quest."

Mildred disappeared in a flash of bright light, leaving the group in the darkness of the cave. Nikolai looked at the Gem in his hands, grateful for this small victory.

"Wow, okay," Finnick said, amazed at what just happened. "So, how do we get out of here?"

"Good question," Iris said looking around.

The group was interrupted by a loud noise. Turning around they saw a door opening within the cave. Light shone through, lighting up the whole area. With the exit clear in view, Finnick bolted towards the exit.

"Yes, freedom!"

The other's followed behind Finnick, relieved to be getting out of the cave's darkness. But Finnick stopped at the door and turned around as he realised Matthew and Simon were still standing at the pedestal.

"Why are you not coming?" Finnick asked confused.

"The exit is here," Omari told Matthew.

Matthew and Simon shared a look.

"We were only meant to help you get out of the cave," Simon said.

"And to assist you with the riddles," Matthew added.

"But you can't stay here, you'll be trapped." Finnick said.

"Don't worry about us. We will be heading home," Simon said.

"Home?" Omari questioned.

Matthew pointed up towards the sky and smiled.

"Safe travels, we will see you again," Matthew said before disappearing.

"Hopefully not too soon," Simon said, waving before he disappeared as well.

The group stood in shock and confusion, as it sunk in as to who Simon and Matthew really were. Their shock turned into amazement.

"Wow," Iris said amazed.

"I cannot believe it," Juliet said, laughing.

"Me too," Nikolai said hugging his wife.

Nikolai, taking Juliet's hand, walked out of the cave followed by Iris, while Finnick and Omari stood in shock as to what they had just witnessed.

"So, just to get this straight, I was saved by a ghost who then helped us escape?" Finnick asked.

"Not a ghost, more like a good spirit," Omari laughed as Finnick shivered.

"Let's get out of here," Finnick told Omari, as they both exited the cave.

Chapter Fourteen

"Blessed are the merciful, for they will be shown mercy."

Matthew 5:7

As Finnick exited the cave, he was glad to leave it, and its riddles behind.

"Ah, sweet fresh air," he breathed, taking in a deep breath, then let out a laugh.

"I second that," Omari laughed along with him.

"It wasn't that bad," Iris told both men. "Was it?" She looked to Juliet and Nikolai in question.

"I say we did pretty well," Nikolai said smiling at his wife.

"Me too. As a team we got in and out pretty quickly, and we got the Crystal Gem," Juliet said excitedly.

"I agree," Iris said.

Alvina came up to the group and neighed. After seeing Nikolai and Juliet come out of the cave, Nix ran up to them and jumped around them playfully, barking with enthusiasm.

"It's good to see you again Nix," Juliet said patting the wolf.

"I hope you haven't been troubling our host," Nikolai said

patting Nix's head.

Alvina smiled and nuzzled the wolf, while Nix licked Alvina's nose playfully. Then Alvina turned and neighed to Iris.

"Congratulations young travellers," Iris interpreted. "Where is the Crystal Gem?"

"Here," Nikolai said walking up to the alicorn.

The alicorn touched the tip of her horn onto the Crystal Gem, and the Gem shrunk to a normal size.

"Wow," Iris gasped. "Neat trick."

"It's beautiful," Omari said.

"It's bright," Finnick said rubbing his eyes.

"Now we need to teach you how to use its power, King Nikolai," Iris interpreted for Alvina. "But for now rest, you've earned it."

"How's the Captain?" Finnick blurted out, suddenly remembering.

"I'm okay," Oberon called out, wincing in pain.

Finnick looked past Alvina and saw his Captain sitting on a large boulder near Crystal Lake. Finnick smiled and waved as he walked over to greet him but stopped suddenly when he saw who was next to him. Standing next to his Captain was Jarreth, alive and well. Finnick choked back tears, marvelled that he was seeing his brother alive. Jarreth smiled at him and waved.

"Jarreth," Finnick whispered in disbelief.

Jarreth smiled and waved at his friend, beckoning him over.

"Your alive," Finnick said laughing.

"Captain Oberon's alive?" Iris asked.

"Iris," Finnick choked back tears. Unable to speak clearly, he just pointed to where Iris needed to look.

"What is it?" she asked.

Iris walked towards Finnick looking past Alvina and saw what Finnick was seeing.

"Jarreth," Iris whispered, hand to her heart.

"*Hey*," Jarreth signed.

Iris held her hands over her mouth to try and keep herself from breaking down in front of everyone. But that all went out the window when Jarreth smiled and opened his arms out to Iris, inviting her into a hug. She ran up to him, tears streaming down her face and hugged him tightly in a loving embrace.

"I thought I lost you," Iris continued to cry.

Jarreth held her tightly as she hugged him back, relieved that she felt something towards him. Pulling apart Iris looked up at Jarreth and smiled as he wiped her tears away.

"It's really you. You're here?" Iris said caressing his face.

"*Yes, I am. I'm not going anywhere,*" he signed, reaching to hold her hand.

Deciding to give his friends a moment together, Finnick walked over to his Captain and smiled.

"You okay Cap?" Finnick asked.

"Yes, I am. But I wouldn't be, if Jarreth hadn't turned up when he did," Oberon said.

"We were all worried about you," Nikolai said joining in the conversation. "Glad to have you back with us Oberon."

"Glad to be back, Your Highness," Oberon said smiling, then winced in pain.

"You're hurt, I'll get Juliet," Nikolai said looking around for her.

After spotting her with Amisha, Nikolai walked over and whispered to her. "Oberon is in need of your healing abilities."

"Of course," Juliet said, following her husband.

Walking back to Oberon, Nikolai saw that Jarreth and Iris had finished their moment together and were talking and laughing with Finnick.

"Glad to have you back with us. You were missed by all,"

Nikolai said to Jarreth.

"*Thanks, Your Highness,*" Jarreth signed.

"Especially by Iris," Juliet said smiling at Iris, who was now blushing at the comment.

Jarreth smiled down at her.

"I know I didn't know you well enough, but I'm glad your back," Omari said.

Jarreth gave Omari a friendly side hug and smiled at his friends.

"I'm glad you're alive," Finnick said. "You're like a brother to me."

"*As are you,*" Jarreth signed to Finnick. "*What did I miss?*"

As the others filled Jarreth in on what had happened since the attack on Iris's kingdom, Juliet went over to Oberon and inspected his wound.

"How are you doing, Captain?" Juliet asked.

"It's going to take a lot more than a snake to put me down. But I am relieved that Jarreth showed up when he did," Oberon said, wincing. "If it's okay with Your Highness, can you heal my stomach? That anaconda ended up binding me up quite tightly, and I think something may be fractured or bruised."

"Of course," Juliet said, sitting on the boulder beside Oberon.

As Juliet began to heal Oberon's wounds, the other's gathered around as Alvina had a message to share. Alvina began to neigh towards Iris who listened carefully before sharing with the group what the alicorn had said to her.

"Tomorrow, they want to start training King Nikolai with the Crystal Gem. But for now, they want us to rest and they will prepare dinner for us," Iris interpreted for Alvina.

"Who's going to teach the King?" Finnick asked.

"I will," Iris said. "Meaning Alvina, not me."

"You are all quite welcome to stay here until the King is able to control the Gem," Iris interpreted for Alvina.

"I'll stay, but I want to send a letter to Theo and my mother explaining everything that's happened so far," Juliet said.

"We'll all stay," Oberon spoke for the group. "It's our duty to protect the King and Queen, and as friends, we'll help out where needed."

"I knew he had a soft spot," Juliet and Iris chuckled to each other.

"I have no idea what you're talking about," Oberon said ignoring the comment, but let a small smile loose to Iris and Juliet.

Alvina neighed to the other alicorn's that had surrounded them. The group looked to Iris for answers but waited as Iris listened to the alicorn. Once Alvina had finished speaking, all the different alicorn's went away to do what they had been asked to do. Iris turned to the group and explained to them what she had just heard.

"Alvina just asked them to get refreshments and food for us," Iris told them. "And to also prepare some bedding for us."

"Um, I hate to sound dumb, but how are they going to do that?" Finnick asked, looking around.

Amisha neighed then came up and nuzzled her head against Juliet, who in return, gave her a pat.

"Hello girl," Juliet greeted, patting Amisha's head before resuming her healing duties.

"Amisha said, they use their horn's magic to do things for humans," Iris explained, patting Amisha's head.

"Neat trick," Finnick said looking around.

"There. All done," Juliet said standing up. "How do you feel?"

Oberon stood up and stretched his body. "Thanks, Your Highness, I feel a lot better."

"You're welcome," Juliet beamed.

Alvina came over to Iris and gave her a rug to spread out for the group to sit on. Once the rug was down the others sat down and talked amongst each other. Nix came up and laid next to Nikolai and Juliet and fell asleep. Amisha trotted over to Nikolai with a white beaded necklace and dropped it into his lap. Nikolai looked up and smiled at the alicorn.

"Thanks Amisha," Nikolai said looking at the beads. "But pearls don't suit me."

Amisha neighed and stomped her hooves as Iris laughed.

"What did I say?" Nikolai asked.

"The necklace helps you to understand Alvina when she trains you," Iris said. "It's a necklace because Amisha wants it to go to Juliet after, so they can communicate in the future."

"Right. I knew that," Nikolai laughed.

"At least I can finally have a break from interpreting," Iris told the group.

"Thanks Amisha," Nikolai said putting the necklace on.

"Training starts at dawn tomorrow," Amisha told Nikolai.

"Thanks," Nikolai said patting her head.

Amisha walked over to Nix and nuzzled the wolf, before lying beside him to rest. Juliet smiled at the two getting along and were grateful for both.

"So how did you manage to survive the fall?" Omari asked, intrigued.

"*The God of Light saved me. Malachi said that I was still needed here, so he healed all my wounds,*" Jarreth told the group. "*I ended up climbing out of the pit and went back to the campsite, because I hadn't seen anyone in the kingdom yet. Queen Athena told me where you were headed, so I came as soon as I could.*"

"And right on time," Oberon said nodding.

"You met with Malachi?" Nikolai asked, shocked.

Jarreth nodded. "*You know him?*"

"He came to us with Mildred and Amisha. He shared some

important information about the Prince of Darkness," Nikolai replied.

"Bless him," Juliet said. "Still helping us even when he's not here."

"I'm more shocked at the fact that someone would give themselves to the Prince of Darkness as an experiment. Being able to turn into an anaconda, it's just wrong," Iris said with disgust.

"People will do pretty much anything to gain power," Oberon sighed sadly.

"The Prince of Darkness must have been pretty convincing," Iris said concerned.

"Most of the time the Prince of Darkness targets people who are weak, desperate, or come from a broken background," Juliet said. "So, they'll pretty much believe anything he tells them."

"It's sad to think there are people out there who don't know the God of Light, and how good he is," Nikolai said with sympathy.

"That's true," Jarreth signed.

The group was interrupted by a group of alicorn's, who came up to them with baskets magically hanging in front of them. The alicorn's placed the baskets onto the ground in front of the group and neighed before leaving.

"Thank you," Finnick called after them.

"What did they say?" Omari asked.

"Enjoy, and call if you need anything else," Iris said picking up a basket.

"Thank you," Omari called out to them.

The group put the baskets in front of them and started laying out all the fruits and cheese's they were given onto the rug. Oberon then took a bottle of wine and began pouring drinks for everyone.

"Thank you," Juliet said, taking the cup Oberon offered her.

"Thanks," Iris said to Oberon.

Once everyone was given a cup of wine and some food, Oberon

cleared his throat and held his cup up to indicate he wanted to speak.

"To the God of Light, and our victory in the Kingdom of Kudzu, and to our victory in Mount Solana. To our friends and family, and may King Nikolai succeed in obtaining the Crystal Gem's power for the sake of the world," Oberon toasted, raising his drink in the air.

"Amen," the group said together, as they raised their own cups in the air.

Nikolai smiled then drank from his cup. He was starting to feel the pressure that came from obtaining the Crystal Gem. He needed to succeed, in order for his family, friends, and subjects, to live peacefully. If not, the world would be doomed to darkness, pain, and slavery.

CHAPTER FIFTEEN

"Anyone who has been stealing must steal no longer, but must work.
Doing something useful with their own hands,
that they may have something to share with those in need."

Ephesians 4:28

Claud looked at the sapphire Gem in his hands and was amazed that healing abilities came from such a small Gem. Movement from below caught his attention. He looked down and saw soldiers from Elaxon searching the area for him. Well, the wolf part of him. He put the sapphire Gem back into his pocket as he watched the soldiers down below. This Gem must be worth a lot if the King and Queen of Elaxon still had soldiers searching for the thief. Claud watched them as they continued further, then he slowly and quietly climbed down the tree and pretended to be another civilian.

"You there," a soldier called out.

Claud sighed to himself before turning around to face the soldier. A flash of panic crossed his face as he realised it was Captain Issac calling out to him.

"Have you seen a wolf pass through here?" Issac asked.

Claud contemplated whether he should kill Issac now, or later when the Prince of Darkness started his war. He saw Issac's soldiers from the corner of his eye and thought later would be best.

"No, I haven't," Claud replied.

"It's dangerous in the forest now. Head back to town until we find this wolf," Issac advised.

"Yes sir," Claud said.

Walking in the direction to the village, Claud saw that Issac's soldiers were watching him suspiciously. Passing by the soldiers, Claud feared that they knew he was the wolf thief they were looking for. His doubts were gone when he passed by them without question. But Claud was annoyed at the fact that he had to walk all the way back into town just to get them off his trail. He would have to lay low for a while before leaving the village, or he could try catching a ride with another civilian who would be heading out of the kingdom soon.

It was just after dawn when Claud entered the village, as the residents were just getting their shops and markets ready for the day. Looking around he saw a civilian packing up a wagon, so Claud walked straight over to the man.

"Hello sir," Claud said, putting on his best smile.

"Hi," the villager greeted suspiciously "How can I help you?"

"Just looking for transport out of Elaxon," Claud said, showing the man some money.

"Where are you headed?" the villager asked.

"To my sister's place, in the country," Claud lied.

"I'm heading to Ashmore, so you can ride with me until then," the villager offered. "I leave in about half an hour."

"Thanks," Claud said, giving the man the money he had.

The villager nodded then continued to pack his wagon.

Walking around to the back, Claud jumped up and sat down at the back and waited for the villager to finish. Once the villager was ready, they set off for Ashmore.

"You're welcome to sit up here. I know it's a little crowded back there," the villager offered.

"I'm good," Claud replied.

Claud stayed hidden in the back of the wagon as the man nodded to the soldiers he passed by, who were coming back from their hunt, unsuccessful.

"Be careful out there, we haven't found the rouge wolf," one of the soldiers advised.

"Will do," the man replied nodding.

Once they were out of the village and on the outskirts of the Kingdom of Elaxon, only then did Claud relax a bit.

Theo paced around Nikolai's office waiting for his brother to return from his errand. Theo was anxious ever since he had received a letter from Queen Julia. What it said concerned him greatly and he needed to let King Nikolai know before it was too late. They were now on a time limit. When Theo heard someone knocking on the office door, he immediately opened it and let them in.

"Fitzwilliam," Theo said, ushering his brother into the room.

"What's wrong brother?" Fitzwilliam asked.

"I just received a letter from Queen Julia," Theo said pacing the office again.

"What does it say?" Fitzwilliam asked.

"Their kingdom's Gem has been stolen. Issac suspects a follower of the Prince of Darkness," Theo said gravely.

"Oh, that's bad," Fitzwilliam said, worriedly.

"It gets worse brother. Their Gem has the power to heal. So, if that Gem gets back to the Prince of Darkness, he will use it to regain his full strength, and break free from the prison the God of Light put him in. Then war will follow soon after," Theo explained.

"Have they caught the follower?" Fitzwilliam asked.

"No, they fled the night after they attacked the Queen and Captain Issac," Theo said, sighing.

Fitzwilliam sighed with his brother. "You are right then, war is coming."

"I'm afraid so," Theo said sadly. "Any news from you or your spy?"

"Yes but it's not good. There have been lots of people disappearing near and around the cave of Akuma, and people are starting to think it's haunted," Fitzwilliam said.

"Why does that place sound familiar?" Theo asked.

"Because as stories go, the cave of Akuma was where the God of Light trapped the Prince of Darkness thousands of years ago."

"Oh, no," Theo said with dread.

Fitzwilliam nodded grimly. "I better get back to work and make sure we have enough weapons and armour."

"Yes, that's a good idea. I'll send word to the King," Theo said sitting at the desk. "Thanks brother, and be careful."

Fitzwilliam nodded then left the room.

Theo took out a pen and paper and started to construct a letter to Nikolai, hoping it would reach him in time. Once done he exited the office and went straight to the soldier's barracks. While walking down the palace hallway he spotted Lord Hain who was in charge while Captain Oberon was away.

"Lord Hain," Theo greeted.

"Advisor Theo how are you today?" Lord Hain asked.

"Not good. I just received word from the Queen of Elaxon. Their healing Gem has been stolen, likely by a follower of the

Prince of Darkness," Theo explained.

Lord Hain sighed. "War is coming then," he asked.

Theo nodded. "Yes, I'm afraid so."

"I'll make sure my men are ready and we'll keep an eye out for anything suspicious," Lord Hain said.

"Thank you," Theo said. "Excuse me, I must go and send this letter to the King."

Theo bowed and continued to walk towards the kingdom's bird aviary. Once he arrived, he looked around for Pete. He was the kingdom's bird keeper. He would look after the birds by feeding them and caring for them. He was also in charge of sending out letters for the King, and notifying him of any incoming letters.

"Pete," Theo called.

"Out back," Pete called back.

Theo walked over to where Pete had called from and found him watching a couple of eggs.

"How can I help you, Advisor Theo?" Pete asked.

"I need you to send this letter for me please," Theo said, handing Pete the letter.

"Who's it going to?" Pete asked, still watching the eggs.

"The King," Theo replied.

"Ah, I know the perfect bird to help you out," Pete said, walking back into the aviary.

"Really?" Theo said sceptical.

"Yes," Pete laughed. "I made it my life goal to train every single one of these birds, no matter the size or species."

"Okay, I trust you" Theo said.

Pete opened one of the cages and put his hand inside, the falcon hopped up onto his hand and Pete brought it out of its cage.

"I trained this falcon to find and deliver messages to the King," Pete said, placing the falcon on the table. "He's been delivering letters to King Nikolai for years."

Pete folded the letter Theo had given him and attached it to the falcon's leg. He then put his hand out for the falcon, and the falcon climbed on. After giving a little whistle Pete released the falcon.

"That's it?" Theo asked dumbly.

"That's it," Pete laughed.

CHAPTER SIXTEEN

"Because of the Lord's great love, we are not consumed,
for his compassions never fail. They are new every morning;
great is your faithfulness."

Lamentations 3:22-23

Nikolai panted with exhaustion as he held onto his sword. Training with his kingdom's topaz Gem had been hard, but training with the Crystal Gem was even harder. Nikolai felt drained every time he tried to use the Gems powers. The first time he had tried to use the power, he immediately passed out and Juliet had to heal him back to full strength, before Alvina would let him try again. After that, he only lasted for about five minutes, which Alvina said was an improvement. Alvina left little room for rest as the days passed by. Every time Nikolai went to bed in the evening, the minute his head hit the pillow, he passed out from exhaustion. But Nikolai wouldn't give up. This was the Prince of Darkness's only weakness, and he had to master it, in order to defeat him and have peace within the kingdoms again.

"Try it again," Alvina said, for what felt like the hundredth time that day.

Nikolai listened to the alicorn and focused on the power of the Crystal Gem. At that moment his sword felt different, lighter somehow.

"Open your eyes slowly while concentrating on the power," Alvina advised.

Nikolai opened his eyes slowly and saw that his sword was glowing a soft white colour on the blade.

"That is what you want your sword to do, with ease and without much concentration. Because when you're in a fight, you have no time to concentrate on getting the Crystal Gem to activate," Alvina explained.

"I understand," Nikolai said.

"Try cutting down the tree behind you," Alvina directed.

Nikolai turned to face the tree the alicorn had referred to. With a swing of his sword, he sliced it in half with little effort. Nikolai stared at it in wonder. The Crystal Gem made his sword feel so much lighter, but it felt powerful at the same time.

"That is the power of the Crystal Gem. It is light but also powerful. Once you strike the Prince of Darkness in the heart with the Crystal Gem, it will turn him to dust," Alvina told him.

"That's it," Nikolai said bewildered.

"Striking the Prince of Darkness in the heart is no easy task. He is skilled in battle, and you must be wary. He will cheat and lie and try to manipulate you to let your guard down. You must be careful," Alvina cautioned.

"Why didn't someone use the sword, and turn the Prince of Darkness to dust all those years ago when he was free?" Nikolai asked.

"The sword was created after the God of Light trapped the Prince of Darkness in the cave. If the Prince of Darkness should ever be freed, the God of Light wanted humanity to have a fighting chance to win," Alvina explained.

Nikolai suddenly collapsed to one knee. The Crystal Gem deactivated, and his sword fell to the ground. He felt dizzy and weak. He focused on his breathing and tried to catch his breath.

"We will stop for today. Get some rest, we'll continue training tomorrow," Alvina said, nodding at Nikolai before turning away.

Juliet, who was watching Nikolai train from a distance, ran over to him and started healing him.

"Thanks," Nikolai said, collapsing to the ground.

"Anytime. I'm proud of you. You managed to get control of the Crystal Gem," Juliet praised him.

"Only for a short time," Nikolai said smiling.

"It still counts, you've been at it for days," Juliet said.

Amisha came up to them and placed a basket full of fruits and nuts in front of them both.

"Thank you, Amisha," Juliet said.

Amisha neighed then sat with them on the grass. Nix followed behind and laid down next to Amisha.

"She says your welcome," Nikolai translated for Juliet.

Juliet smiled at Amisha then gave Nix a good pat.

"And where have you been Nix, you've been missing for days," Juliet said.

"Probably off hunting somewhere," Nikolai said sitting up and patting Nix.

"How's the training going?" Oberon asked, with Jarreth and Iris in tow.

"Difficult, but slowly getting there," Nikolai said.

"He managed to control the Crystal Gem through his sword," Juliet praised.

"Only for a short while," Nikolai said covering his yawn.

"Hey, it's progress," Oberon said, picking up an apple and biting into it.

"That's still good, as Gems can be difficult to master," Iris said, sitting down with Jarreth beside her.

"I agree, it took me a month to heal a soldier's injury," Juliet said.

"A soldier's injury," Iris laughed. "Do tell the story."

Juliet smiled then spoke. "When I first started practising with my Gem, my mother would get me to heal different soldier's wounds. They didn't mind because it meant they could get back to work quicker, instead of being bedridden till their injures healed."

"*I guess it helped both you and them*," Jarreth signed, smiling.

"It did, a lot," Juliet replied.

Jarreth held up one finger to signal "Wait a minute" while he dug into his pocket, trying to find something.

"What's wrong?" Iris asked.

"*This*," Jarreth signed, holding up a light brown Gem with bits of gold inside.

"What is it?" Nikolai asked.

"Can I have a closer look?" Iris asked.

Jarreth gave the Gem to Iris as he began to explain to the others how he had gotten it. "*I found it on Anna when the Captain and I defeated her.*"

"Do you think she stole it or actually completed a quest for it?" Juliet asked.

"*Don't know*," Jarreth shrugged.

"This here," Iris said, holding the Gem up with excitement. "Is a Brown Goldstone."

"Really," Juliet asked.

"I'm serious," Iris said.

"Um, care to fill us in on it powers," Nikolai said.

"Sorry," Iris said touching Jarreth's arm. "King Nikolai, Captain Oberon, do you remember when we crossed the pond before entering into Amisha's home?"

"Yes," Oberon said confused.

"Did any of you see Anna before that?" Iris asked, looking to both men.

"No, why?" Nikolai said.

"A massive anaconda that no one saw, who we now realize, owned this Gem," Iris said, holding it up to show them.

"*Camouflage?*" Jarreth questioned.

"YES!!!" Iris exclaimed.

"The Gem has the ability to camouflage the user," Nikolai said as it sunk in.

"Yes," Iris said giving it back to Jarreth. "I'll teach you, if you like."

"*Thank you,*" Jarreth signed smiling.

"That's going to be quite handy in the war," Oberon voiced.

"It will be," Nikolai said, nodding to Jarreth. "Good find."

Once Juliet was finished healing Nikolai, the others came to share the food Amisha had brought for all of them.

"Guys," Finnick hollered, walking up to them with Omari behind him.

"What's wrong?" Nikolai asked concerned.

"Alvina said there was a messenger bird outside near the waterfall, so she let me out to retrieve this," Finnick said, handing the letter to Nikolai.

"It's from Theo, I recognise our kingdom's falcon," Finnick said, sitting down and helping himself to some fruit.

"I hope it's not bad news," Iris said with concern.

Nikolai opened the letter and read the contents inside to himself. The others waited patiently as their King read in silence, hoping, and praying for good news.

"So," Finnick said, trying to sound casual.

Nikolai read the letter one last time before putting it down, then he sighed.

"That bad?" Oberon asked.

"It's from Queen Julia." Nikolai said.

"Is she-" Juliet began.

"She and Issac are fine. But she says her kingdom's Gem has been stolen. Most likely by a follower of the Prince of Darkness," Nikolai told the group.

"Oh no," Juliet said with dread. "If the Prince of Darkness gets that Gem, he will be able to have the strength to break free from his prison."

"So, we are on a time limit now," Oberon said gravely, folding his arms as he thought to himself.

"It seems so," Nikolai said, thinking.

"What's on your mind?" Omari asked Nikolai.

Nikolai looked around at his friends and family.

"I think we need to start planning for the war. We notify each kingdom about the current situation. Then we all meet up at a location that is to our advantage, and together we stand up against the Prince of Darkness," Nikolai advised.

"I think that is wise" Oberon agreed.

"Do we know where the Prince of Darkness is hiding?" Omari asked.

"I was just informed that there have been many disappearances around the cave of Akuma," Nikolai said.

"The cave of Akuma," Oberon said shocked.

"Isn't that where the God of Light trapped the Prince of Darkness thousands of years ago?" Juliet asked.

"I thought that was a myth," Finnick said stunned.

"It makes sense that he's hiding there. Akuma means darkness," Oberon said thinking to himself. "I can't believe we didn't think of it sooner."

"To be fair, we have had a lot on our minds. We've been dealing with the creatures of darkness. It's no wonder it slipped our minds," Juliet explained.

"Maybe it was the Prince of Darkness's goal to send his creatures out to distract us from his hideout, so he could plan his war without any distractions," Nikolai said thinking. "Think about it, we were all so focused on our own kingdoms, that when our own kingdom was safe, we went to help others who were still under siege." Nikolai nodded towards Omari and Iris.

"It would make sense," Iris said. "Using Jorogumo as a distraction."

"Smart move," Omari said." Getting us all distracted from the real goal."

"Princess Iris, you head back to your kingdom and explain the situation to your mother. Start planning with her Highness and the Captain. In three days, we will meet up near the cave of Akuma."

"Will do," Iris nodded.

"Juliet, you take Amisha and fly to your home kingdom. Let your mother know the situation and inform Captain Issac. Meet up with Princess Iris and her troops in three days."

"Okay," Juliet replied.

"Omari, you fly back to your kingdom and let your father know we need him and his troops for war," Nikolai said. "Meet up with the others in three days."

"Of course," Omari nodded.

"Finnick, Jarreth you head back to the Kingdom of Zolatta and help Theo and Lord Hain prepare for war," Nikolai said. "Meet up with the others in three days."

"Done," Finnick replied.

Jarreth nodded.

"I will stay here and continue to learn how to control the Crystal Gem. I'll meet up with all of you on the battlefield. Oberon you stay here in case I need your assistance," Nikolai said.

"Done," Oberon said to Nikolai, then he turned to Juliet. "I'll keep him safe, Queen Juliet. I promise."

"Thank you, Captain," Juliet said.

"Alright, in three days we meet up near the cave of Akuma. We stop the Prince of Darkness together. If anything happens before we meet up that is not according to plan, contact one another and let us know," Nikolai told the group.

"Agreed," they all replied.

"Princess Iris, can you organise animals that can blend or camouflage to watch the cave of Akuma and its dealings. If things move quicker or slower you can let us know," Nikolai asked.

"Of course," Iris nodded.

"Okay," Nikolai breathed. "Rest up and make your preparations to leave tomorrow morning."

◆ ◆ ◆ ◆ ◆

Once the villager had stopped the wagon for the night, Claud waited until he was sound asleep before making his move. Once Claud heard snoring, he got up quietly and left on foot, leaving the villager and his wagon behind. Once he had gotten a good mile away, he looked around to see if there was anyone else nearby. Satisfied that he was alone he turned and ventured into the forest. Once he was deep enough, he began to transform into a wolf. When the change was complete, Claud let out a long howl and started running deeper into the forest in the direction of the cave of Akuma, his master's hideout. The wind on his fur was a cold sensation as he ran through the night. The ground was wet from the dew, but Claud kept on running as he was eager to get this Gem to his master. He held onto the sapphire Gem with his teeth, careful not to break or drop it as he ran. The further he ran the more excited he got. Excited that once his master had the Gem and regained his strength and power, Claud would show all those people who had bullied and abused him throughout his life what real pain was. He smiled to himself.

Suddenly, Claud stopped and sniffed the air, tensing at the threat waiting for him. He was a couple of miles out from the cave of Akuma, and he smelt trouble. That trouble was Serpentina.

Something wasn't right.

Why was she waiting outside? Was she waiting for him? Is the master angry?

The thoughts consumed Claud's mind, making him doubtful and wary.

Feeling unsure about what was going to happen, he dropped the sapphire Gem near a large banyan tree, making sure to hide it within the roots so he could find it again later, once the threat passed. Turning around he sniffed the air again and growled. She was still there and waiting. Claud walked toward the cave of Akuma carefully. The closer he got to the cave, the more clearly he could see Serpentina outside the cave in her true form.

The basilisk.

Claud walked up towards her, being careful not to look her in the eyes, otherwise, it would be instant death for him. It's said that one look from a basilisk can kill any living thing. Human or wolf, it didn't matter. Serpentina could still kill him at any given chance.

"Serpintina," Claud growled, lowering his head.

"My my Claud, haven't you been a good boy," Serpentina teased.

"What's going on?" Claud asked. "Have you come to greet me?"

"Where's the Gem?" Serpentina cut to the point.

"I was just about to bring it to the master if you would get out of my way first," Claud said, standing his ground.

"Give me the Gem," Serpentina barked.

"Over my dead body," Claud growled.

"I think that can be arranged," Serpentina laughed.

Serpentina began circling him. He kept his eyes low towards the ground but enough to keep her within view. He saw her snake body slithering around him.

"Last time Claud," Serpentina said. "Where is the Gem?"

"Like I would tell you," Claud fumed, getting angry.

Claud leaped forward and bit down hard onto Serpentina's snake body. She screamed as she tried to shake him off. Serpentina, turning her body around, faced Claud and bit down onto his tail causing him to loosen the hold he had on her. Claud whined as he let go of Serpentina. Suddenly he was being dragged back by Serpentina, who had quickly gotten behind him. Claud struggled to fight her but kept trying to scratch and bite her whenever he could. Using her snake body, Serpentina curled around Claud until he was fully bounded, unable to move.

"Well, aren't we nice and cosy," Serpentina snickered.

Serpentina got close to Claud's face, who now had his eyes closed.

"The Gem?" she asked politely.

Claud didn't say anything.

Serpentina smiled as she began to tighten the grip she had around Claud, causing him to howl in pain.

"The Gem?" Serpentina asked again.

Claud smiled at her but still stood his ground and said nothing.

Serpentina smiled again and tightened her grip on Claud even more so, making some of his bones begin to break.

Claud howled in pain.

"I won't ask again," Serpentina said glaring at Claud.

"I'd love to be a fly on the wall when you tell the master that you lost the sapphire Gem," Claud said letting out a small laugh.

Serpentina hissed at him angrily.

"Fine, have it your way. It must be around here somewhere. I'll just have to find it before I head back inside to the master," Serpentina said.

Serpentina tightened her grip on Claud one last time, as the snapping sound of breaking bones echoed throughout the area. After dropping his broken body to the ground, she slithered off to find the Gem. Claud, unable to do anything, watched as Serpentina slithered away. Before his last breath left him, he hoped she would never find the Gem.

CHAPTER SEVENTEEN

"He said to them,
"Go into all the world and preach the gospel to all creation."

Mark 16:15

"All set?" Nikolai asked his wife as she mounted Amisha.

Juliet nodded and sighed.

"Hey," Nikolai caressed her cheek. "We'll see each other soon."

Juliet nodded as Nikolai leaned up to kiss her.

"I love you," he whispered.

"I love you too," Juliet replied.

"Please look after one another," Nikolai told Juliet and Amisha. "And before you go, Alvina wanted you to have this."

Nikolai gave Juliet the same necklace that allowed him to speak to the alicorn race.

"Tell her I said thank you," Juliet said smiling, as she put on the necklace.

"Will do," Nikolai said.

"Safe travels, Your Highness," Oberon said walking up to

them both. "I will make sure he comes back to you."

"Thanks Captain," Juliet said, then turned to the alicorn. "Ready Amisha?"

"I'm ready," Amisha said, flexing her wings out.

Amisha neighed then began running to build up speed. After expanding her wings, they lifted off the ground and began to glid into the air. Once they reached the maximum safety height, Amisha glided over the alicorn's home and headed towards the Kingdom of Elaxon. Juliet was astonished at the alicorn's ability and flight, and for a moment she was speechless. Amisha smiled at Juliet's reaction, as she let the Queen admire the view and experience before they talked for the first time.

"This is amazing Amisha," Juliet said in wonder. "You are truly magnificent."

"Thank you," Amisha said.

"The view is breathtaking. I can understand why Princess Iris wanted to gain your ability," Juliet said, laughing with her hands in the air.

"She is more than welcome to, all she has to do is ask," Amisha said.

"She'll be happy to hear that," Juliet said, as she patted Amisha.

The two flew towards Juliet's home kingdom. It was just after dawn, and Juliet calculated that they would reach their destination within a few hours, with Amisha's speed and flying. As Juliet soared through the sky, she said a silent prayer for all her friends and family who would participate in this upcoming war. She also prayed for courage and strength to help lead her people through the war. Juliet sighed. She was terrified. Yes, she had been through war before, but even then, she was scared. The only thing that kept her mind occupied was saving her people through her healing.

"Are you okay?" Amisha asked.

"Just thinking," Juliet said sadly. "I had hoped to not experience another war in my lifetime. The first one was hard and now instead of fighting people, we'll be fighting against the Prince of Darkness and his creatures of darkness. It's terrifying."

"It can be pretty terrifying, but you have your friends and family to fight with you, and I will help you as well," Amisha encouraged.

"Thank you, Amisha," Juliet said, hugging her alicorn.

After flying for a few hours Juliet could see the Kingdom of Elaxon in the distance and immediately got homesick. She hadn't been back in a while and realised she missed her mother terribly.

"We're almost there," Amisha said seeing the kingdom too.

As they both flew over the outskirts of the kingdom, villagers looked up amazed at what they were seeing. Juliet smiled and waved down at her people.

"It's Queen Juliet," a villager exclaimed.

Once Amisha and Juliet landed at the palace, Juliet dismounted and ran to her mother, who was waiting on the palace steps with Issac, with her arms outstretched.

"Juliet, I missed you," Queen Julia said, hugging her daughter. "My guards saw you flying over the kingdom and informed me right away."

"I missed you too mother," Juliet said. "Sorry I didn't write; it's been a busy couple of weeks."

"It's okay," Queen Julia said.

"It's good to see you again, Juliet," Issac greeted, holding out his hand.

"You too Issac," Juliet said, giving him a quick hug which he returned.

Juliet turned back to Amisha and went over to the alicorn.

"This is Amisha," Juliet introduced.

"She's beautiful. Look at her wings," Queen Julia admired.

Amisha neighed and held her head high with her wings outstretched, which glittered in the sun.

"A majestic creature indeed."

"Where is King Nikolai?" Issac asked looking around. "Is he alright?"

Juliet's smile turned into worry.

"Juliet what's wrong?" Queen Julia asked.

"Can we talk somewhere private?" Juliet asked, looking around at the villagers gathered at the palace gates. "Please."

"Of course," Queen Julia said ushering her inside.

Juliet turned to face Amisha.

"Are you going to be okay," she asked her.

"Go on, I'll be fine. I'm going to look for a nice patch of grass. Call me if you need me, I won't be far," Amisha said trotting off. Juliet turned back to her mother and Issac whose faces were marked with confusion.

"The leader of the alicorn race gave me a necklace so I can communicate with Amisha," Juliet explained, pointing at the necklace.

"We have a lot to catch up on," Queen Julia said as she laughed. Juliet followed her mother and Issac to an outdoor setting inside the palace gardens. Juliet sat down while the maids brought out some sandwiches and tea.

"So, tell me what's been happening," Queen Julia said picking up her tea.

"I'm not sure where to begin. What's the last thing we wrote to you about?" Juliet asked.

"Mildred and Malachi bringing you Amisha," Queen Julia thought out loud.

"No, I believe it was helping Princess Iris take back her kingdom," Issac said to Julia.

"Oh yes, I believe it was. How did that go?" Queen Julia asked with concern.

"We won the battle and defeated Jorogumo and her minions," Juliet said taking a sip of her tea.

"That's good news," Queen Julia said. "How is the kingdom going?"

"They are slowly getting their kingdom back up and running. It might take time, but they will get there," Juliet said with confidence.

"That's a relief," Queen Julia said, hand to her heart. "It must be difficult for them. Can we help in anyway?"

"Maybe, I'm sure they would appreciate the help," Juliet said, as she put her tea down and sighed.

"I'm guessing that's not the reason why you've come home," Queen Julia said.

"What's wrong?" Issac said concerned. "Anyone I need to take care of?"

Juliet chuckled. "No, but thanks."

"What's on your mind Juliet?" Queen Julia asked.

"War is coming. Nikolai sent me here to tell you, and to help you prepare for it," Juillet said worriedly.

"Is it because the sapphire Gem was stolen by one of the Prince of Darkness's followers?" Issac asked.

"Don't put yourself through that Issac. It wasn't your fault," Queen Julia said taking Issac's hand.

"She's right. It's not your fault Issac," Juliet agreed. "It could have happened to me, if Nikolai wasn't with me."

Issac nodded, then looked to both Queens. "So, what's the plan?"

"Nikolai is still with Alvina, the leader of the alicorn race. He's undergoing training to control the Crystal Gem. We are to meet everyone near the cave of Akuma in three days," Juliet explained.

"Alright," Issac nodded thinking. "I will inform my men and

get them ready."

"Great, thank you," Juliet said, then turned to her mother. "I have been given another Gem by a late friend. Will you help me train, so I'm more prepared for the war."

"Of course, sweetheart," her mother said intrigued. "What type of Gem is it?"

"The emerald Gem. It has the ability to control the earth," Juliet explained, taking out the little green Gem.

"We can get started on training tomorrow, but rest today, you've had a long journey," Queen Julia said, offering her daughter a plate of food.

"Thanks mother," Juliet said, taking a sandwich from the offered plate.

CHAPTER EIGHTEEN

"May the God who gives endurance and encouragement give you the same attitude of mind toward each other that Christ Jesus had."

Romans 15:5

Iris was grateful that Prince Omari allowed her to take on his griffin's abilities once again before leaving for his home kingdom. Iris had made it home in half the time because of her wings. Soaring through the sky she was happy and smiling despite the upcoming war. Jarreth was alive and had found his way back to the group which made her blush with excitement.

As Iris flew over the campsite, she began to panic as the place looked chaotic. All the tents were either gone or laid in a heap on the ground broken. Food wrappings littered the ground. There was no one about that Iris could see, and that scared her. Descending, Iris looked around. Fear crept inside her, telling her the worse had happened. Had her people been attacked? Where were they?

As the griffin's abilities wore off, Iris took out her small dagger for protection. She began looking around the deserted campsite, looking under tarps and behind massive trees, but couldn't find a single soul. Just before she lost all hope, she heard someone behind her.

"Princess Iris!"

Turning around, Iris was relieved when she saw Chase, the kingdoms new Captain of the Royal Guard, riding up to her.

"What happened, where is everyone?" Iris asked panicked.

"Back at the kingdom. There was supposed to be a guard still here to let you know when you returned. We weren't sure if you would receive a letter where you were going," Chase said looking around. "I came to relieve the guard of his duty. Where is he?"

"There's no one here," Iris said. "I just checked."

Chase dismounted his horse and drew out his sword, checking the camp and surrounding areas for his fellow soldier. Iris turned and followed close behind with her daggers out and ready to fight if needed. Splitting up from Chase, Iris went to check the table and chairs that were stacked up neatly, as she had missed them before. Iris walked slowly around the chairs that were waiting to be taken back to the kingdom. After finding nothing she turned back around, but something caught her eye just behind the chairs and amongst the trees. Something glittered in the sun. Curious, Iris went to check it out. As she got closer dread filled her. Behind one of the trees, she saw the guard's sword lying on the ground, with blood covering the blade. The hairs on her arm stood up as she suddenly felt exposed in the open. She felt like someone was watching her, from beyond the trees. Turning around she whistled for Chase's attention. Chase came running up to Iris and looked at the sword lying on the ground.

"Where's the body?" Chase asked looking around.

"Chase," Iris whispered.

Chase turned and looked at Iris. She had her hands covering her mouth, as she tried holding back the tears of shock as she pointed up to the trees. Chase followed her gaze to the treetops and found his fallen comrade, hanging from a branch, dead. His body was covered in scratches to the point he was no longer recognisable.

"What on earth did this?" Chase said, covering his nose from the stench.

"I- I don't, I don't know," Iris said.

"Princess, look away, I'll climb up and get him down. Hopefully whatever got him is long gone already," Chase said, ready to climb.

Before Chase could climb the tree, he and Iris heard a low growl coming from somewhere behind them. Turning around they came face to face with an unusual creature. This creature had a lion and a goat's head, and a snake as its tail. It had blood dripping from its mouth and claws. The lion began to growl, and the snake hissed from behind.

"Chase," Iris whispered in fear.

"Yes, Your Highness," Chase said staring at the creature.

"That's no ordinary beast," she whispered. "That's a chimera. They're extremely dangerous."

"I thought they were all destroyed back in the day," Chase whispered back.

"The Prince of Darkness must have brought it back," Iris said.

"He probably heard about the recent victory against Jorogumo," Chase said.

The chimera lunged at Chase but was too late as both Iris and Chase broke apart, fleeing in separate directions, causing the chimera to stumble into the stacked chairs. Iris looked around trying to find a suitable animal to harness their abilities to fight this beast, but to her dismay there were no animals in sight that could defeat it. They had probably all fled in fear of the chimera. Iris gripped her daggers tightly while she watched Chase battle the chimera. She felt useless with them in her hands. The chimera came at Chase again trying to bite and slash at the captain, but Chase kept avoiding its attacks while trying to figure out a way to injure the beast, without getting himself killed in the process. Meanwhile Iris looked around her surroundings, trying to find any animal that would help. Iris quickly checked to see how Chase was doing before she walked to the forests entrance and looked around there. Still nothing. She looked back at Chase and saw him struggling against the beast. Remembering her amphibian friends, she ventured deeper into the forest to find a specific species of frog that would help her defeat the chimera.

Hold on Chase Iris thought.

She walked around the forest listening quietly, hoping she could find what she was looking for. She stopped as she heard a familiar sound. Near the waterfall sitting on a rock, she saw a golden poison dart frog, croaking. The frog was small and had black markings on its snout. From a distance it looked quite cute, but the small frog was very deadly.

"Yes," Iris cheered. "Thank you, God of Light."

Golden poison dart frogs were extremely poisonous and were lethal to humans and animals. This would defiantly help her and Chase with their beast problem. Iris knelt near the frog, carefully keeping her distance.

"Excuse me," Iris said.

"What," the frog croaked.

"I need your help," Iris said. "And in exchange I will give you food. Spiders to be exact."

The frog turned its attention to her.

"I'm listening," it croaked.

"I need some of your venom?" Iris asked.

"It's very poisonous," it warned.

"I know, I just need to coat my daggers with it," Iris said, taking the weapons out.

"Be careful, Princess," it said.

The frog stood still while Iris gently coated a leaf with the venom then transferred it to her daggers.

"Thank you. The spiders are in my kingdoms dungeon's. I can bring some back once I'm done," Iris said smiling.

"Better keep your word Princess," the frog warned.

"I will."

Iris then turned and ran back towards Chase, keeping the dagger at arm's length, being careful not to get the poison on her. When Iris got back to the camp she saw Chase panting from exhaustion, with the chimera only a few meters in front of him without a scratch. Iris ran towards them. Once she was within distance of the chimera, she threw one of her poison daggers at the beast. The dagger pierced its flesh, triggering a screech from all three animals. The chimera's snake tail pulled the dagger out and threw it on the ground, hissing a warning at Iris.

"I need you to distract it so I can get another shot," Iris shouted.

"But-," Chase began.

"I have a plan," Iris said.

Chase nodded and moved away from Iris. Waving his hands in the air he whistled for the beast's attention.

"Hey," Chase yelled.

The chimera looked towards Chase, hesitating a second before rushing after the captain. While the beast chased the captain, Iris came from behind and threw her dagger again, this time piercing the chimera's leg. After a moment the beast came to a slow pace, with the venom finally taking its toll. The snake removed the second dagger then flopped to the ground, weak from the poison that was now working its way through its system. The chimera howled, its body becoming weaker and weaker till it collapsed to the ground.

"What's happening?" Chase asked, running up to Iris.

"The venom is working. I found a golden poison dart frog in the forest by the stream. I asked for some venom in exchange for food," Iris explained.

"What does it eat?" Chase asked curiously.

"Spiders," Iris said, smiling.

Chase laughed. "At least we don't need to clean up the mess in the dungeons."

"We still need to bring them to him. I don't know how were going to get him there without getting poisoned by accident," Iris said.

"I'm happy to help," Chase said, laughing again.

Iris and Chase both looked towards the beast. It was bleating, growling, and hissing at them from the ground.

"It's not going to survive much longer," Iris pointed out. "It's best we head back. I don't want to be out here when its dark."

"I say we head back to the kingdom and reward our new friend," Chase chuckled. "I'm still amazed by your Gems abilities."

"I am grateful to the God of Light for this wonderful gift," Iris praised.

Leaving the chimera behind, Chase and Iris mounted the horse and made the quick journey back to the kingdom. Once the two had arrived back at the Kingdom of Kudzu, Iris and Chase made a quick stop to the dungeons to retrieve a few of Jorogumo's spiders, to give to their new amphibian friend. Once they returned to their old campsite they found the beast dead. While Chase started a fire to burn the corpse, Iris went into the forest where she met the poison dart frog and knelt to the ground near it.

"You're back," the frog crocked.

"I always keep my word," Iris said smiling. "Plus, you saved mine and my friends life today."

"Well, I'm glad I could help," the frog said.

Iris smiled as she opened the bag that was filled with

Jorogumo's dead minions. Pouring the contents on the ground the frog waited until Iris moved away, before it jumped down into the pile of spiders and began feeding.

"Thanks Princess," the frog said, in between mouthful.

"You're welcome," Iris said, trying to hide her disgust.

After giving the spiders to an incredibly grateful frog, the two headed back to the kingdom as the day came to an end.

"Chase, I know it's been a long day for you, but I need you present when I speak to my mother," Iris asked.

"No problem, Your Highness," Chase said. "I'm Captain of the Royal Guard, it's my duty to serve the throne."

"Thank you," Iris said.

As they entered the Kingdom of Kudzu Iris was speechless. Her people had gathered to help restore their home. They had already begun rebuilding the destroyed houses and buildings. They had cleaned up the streets that were previously filled with debris from Jorogumo's reign. Others were busy planting fresh flowers, shrubs, and trees, which brought some wildlife back into the area. Even the animals that lived within the kingdom freely, were helping. Horses were pulling wagons filled with debris, dogs of all breeds were picking up rocks, sticks, branches, and old broken wood from buildings. Tigers were picking up the dead carcasses that lay across the street and took them away from the kingdom where they would be burned. Iris was almost in tears as she watched her people and the animals help one another. Even though her people couldn't communicate with the animals, anyone who lived in the Kingdom of Kudzu had a special bond with one.

A bond of friendship that would last a lifetime.

Iris and Chase dismounted their horse, and walked up the palace steps to where Queen Athena and some birds were removing the cobwebs that surrounded the palace.

"There's one more piece to your left," Queen Athena told the bird.

The bird flew to where Athena pointed and removed the cobweb.

"Thank you, my friend," she called out.

The bird replied with tweets and chirps, as Athena looked up with sadness.

"I'm sorry my friend, I cannot understand you anymore. I no longer have my Gem," Queen Athena's voice broke.

Iris went up to her mother and hugged her side on, as she laid her head on her shoulder.

"They said they are happy to help because it means they can come home. You know, even though you cannot understand them, they will always understand you and help you whenever needed," Iris interpreted for her mother. "After when the war is over, we can venture into the forest and retrieve another Gem for you."

"Thank you my dear," Queen Athena said, hugging her daughter back. "Is everything okay, you're back early. It's only been a couple of days since you left."

"I need a word with you and Chase," Iris asked her mother.

"Of course," Queen Athena said.

Queen Athena, Princess Iris, and Captain Chase all walked into the palace and into one of the sitting rooms that had been cleaned out. They sat down and waited for Princess Iris to speak.

"We found the Crystal Gem, which is the Prince of Darkness's weakness," Iris said happily.

"Oh, that's such great news," Queen Athena beamed. "There were no casualties?"

"No casualties," Iris said smiling and blushing. "Jarreth is alive. The God of Light saved him. Thank you for letting him know where we were, if it weren't for him, Captain Oberon wouldn't be alive."

"I'm happy to help, we don't need any more deaths," Queen Athena said thinking of her husband.

Iris agreed with her mother, also thinking of her father.

"King Nikolai is currently training with the alicorn leader to use the Gem. But halfway during his training we were notified that the healing Gem from the Kingdom of Elaxon had been stolen. If the Prince of Darkness gets it, he will regain his full power sooner," Iris explained.

"So, war is coming," Chase said grimly.

"Yes, I'm afraid so. King Nikolai sent me back to inform you and to help prepare our people for war. We are to meet the other kingdoms and their army near the cave of Akuma in three days," Iris told them.

"What if the Prince of Darkness moves earlier?" Queen Athena asked.

"King Nikolai has asked me to send some birds to keep watch. If the Prince of Darkness does move before then, we will notify everyone," Iris explained.

"Smart move," Queen Athena said, smiling at her daughter.

Chase sighed. "I will inform my men and get them prepared."

"Thank you, Captain," Queen Athena thanked.

"And I will see if we can get our animal friends to help," Iris said standing up. "I'll be back in time for dinner mother."

"Okay, be careful," Queen Athena said.

"I promise," Iris said hugging her mother.

CHAPTER NINETEEN

"Do not take revenge, my dear friends, but leave room for God's wrath, for it is written: 'It is mine to avenge; I will repay,' says the Lord."

Romans 12:19

Omari flew above the forest near his home, feeling free and full of energy. He was happy he had made a lot of new friends and experienced a lot of new things. But sad and angry that war was coming. He knew that loss and sacrifice were a part of war, and was scared, having never been through a war in his life.

Landing just outside the forest, Omari began changing back to human. Once the transformation was complete, he dressed in the spare clothes King Nikolai gave him and began walking towards his home. Omari walked through his kingdoms front gate and smiled. It was good to be back. The townspeople were all rushing around at the morning markets as Omari strolled into town. Market stalls stood prepped and ready with customers already lining up for goods. Kids took part in a game of tug of war in the corner streets without a care in the world. The aroma of fresh bread filled Omari with hunger, so he stood in line waiting to be served.

"Breakfast," a familiar voice interrupted Omari's thought of food.

Turning around Omari saw Kirsten, his father's Captain of the Royal Guard, smiling at him.

"Ca- Captain," Omari stumbled on his words. "What are you doing here?"

"Patrolling. We have had a lot of creature sightings lately," Kirsten said as she smiled at him. "But none have come close to the kingdom, thankfully."

"That's good," Omari beamed.

Omari met Kirsten when she was promoted as the new Captain and they instantly clicked. Omari had always liked Kirsten because she never judged Omari with his curse. They spent a lot of time together training. King Jabari wanted his son to be able to fight and defend himself without using his curse. So, Kirsten was Omari's only friend here in the kingdom, before he went traveling.

"It's good to see you're back. Your father told me where you were going and what you were doing," Kirsten said.

"He did?" Omari said anxiously.

"Of course, I am the captain. My job is to protect the throne, and that includes you," she said. "Why are you back so early, has something happened?"

"Yes, I need to speak with my father and yourself, Captain," Omari said, paying for the fresh bread before continuing to the palace.

"Of course," Kirsten said with concern, as she followed him.

Omari tried to hide his concern with a smile, then answered. "Great."

Together they walked up the palace steps and towards King

Jabari's office. Once they were in front of the door, Omari knocked and waited to be invited in by the King.

"Come in," King Jabari called out.

Omari and Kirsten walked into the Kings office and bowed.

"Son," King Jabari greeted, walking up and hugging him.

"Hey dad," Omari said returning the hug.

"How were your travels? To be honest I thought you'd be gone longer. But I'm glad your back and so will your mother," King Jabari said sitting back down.

"I met with the King and Queen of Zolatta. They told me that in order to be free of this curse, the caster must be defeated," Omari told his father.

"Do they know who cursed you in the first place?" King Jabari asked.

"They had a women come to them who switched sides, and she told the Queen that a women named Serpentina put the curse on me," Omari explained.

"So, all we need to do is find this Serpentina, which mind you, is another follower of the Prince of Darkness, who can change into God knows what and judging by her name, I'm guessing it's probably a snake. Then defeat her so you can be curse free," Kirsten thought aloud.

"Yes, that sums it up," Omari said, nodding.

"That is going to be difficult," Kirsten said thinking.

"I didn't say it would be easy," Omari answered.

"Don't give up son, thanks to the King and Queen of Zolatta we now know who cursed you. That's progress," King Jabari comforted his son.

"Thanks dad," Omari replied.

"Kirsten, I want you to now focus on finding this Serpentina, and bring her here," King Jabari ordered.

Both the captain and the King stood up ready to find this

follower and be done with this curse.

"Wait," Omari spoke.

Kirsten and King Jabari looked at Omari with concern.

"What is it, son?" King Jabari asked.

"There's more I need to tell you," Omari sighed.

"More?" King Jabari said, crossing his arms across his chest.

"Father, please sit," Omari gestured to the chair.

King Jabari and Kirsten sat back down and waited patiently for Omari to finish speaking.

"The Prince of Darkness is preparing for war. The healing Gem that the Kingdom of Elaxon owns has been stolen by a follower. When that Gem reaches the Prince of Darkness, he will be able to regain his full strength and break free from the prison, that the God of Light trapped him in thousands of years ago," Omari said, looking at both his father and friend before he continued. "I went and helped King Nikolai find the Crystal Gem. It's the Prince of Darkness's weakness. King Nikolai is currently training to control the Gem in order to defeat the Dark One. He has sent me back home in order to warn you and to prepare for war. We are to meet him and the other kingdoms near the cave of Akuma in three days."

King Jabari stared at his son as he processed the news. He rubbed his chin and sighed, nodding to Kirsten. "Inform your solder's and prepare for war."

"Yes, Your Highness," Kirsten said, standing up and bowing to both before rushing out of the room.

"And what if the Prince of Darkness moves first?" King Jabari asked.

"King Nikolai will send word. He's asked Princess Iris to have birds keep watch over the cave and inform us once they see movement."

"And the training?" King Jabari asked.

"He'll have to make do with the training he's done, and hope to the God of Light that it's enough to defeat the Prince of Darkness," Omari replied, feeling hopeful.

"Let's all pray that he master's the training," King Jabari said sighing.

There was a knock at the door interrupting Omari and his father. Turning around Omari saw his mother and smiled. Queen Nala entered with open arms as she embraced Omari.

"I'm sorry to interrupt but I heard Omari was back," Queen Nala said holding her son.

"It's good to be back. I know I wasn't gone long, but I missed you," Omari said, hugging his mother back.

"How are you, have you eaten, are you hurt?" Queen Nala fussed.

"I'm good mother. I've eaten a little. Father and I were just having a meeting, and I'm not hurt," Omari chuckled at his mother's worry.

Queen Nala looked to her husband with concern.

"War is coming my dear," he said, not bothered to hide his worry.

"War," Queen Nala whispered.

"I'm afraid so," Omari said sadly.

"I was hoping we wouldn't have another in our lifetime," Queen Nala sighed, taking her husbands offered hand. "Who are we going to war with?"

"The Prince of Darkness, his followers, and his creatures of darkness," Omari said, sitting back down, ready to explain to his mother everything that happened on his journey.

"Oh my," Queen Nala said, sitting with her husband, thinking. "I will help prepare for battle."

"Sweetheart," King Jabari began.

"No," Queen Nala stopped her husband. "I can also fight; I

also have our kingdom's Gem power." She showed her husband her ring, reminding him.

"Yes, I know you can fight, believe me," King Jabari said smiling, remembering the last match they had. But then he looked at her with concern. "This time we are going against the Prince of Darkness himself."

"If I recall our last practice session, I believe it was me who won our little match," Queen Nala said smiling at her husband.

King Jabari burst out laughing. "What am I to do with you, my beautiful, strong wife." King Jabari picked up her hand and kissed it.

CHAPTER TWENTY

*"Ask and it will be given to you, seek and you will find,
knock and the door will be opened to you."*

Matthew 7:7

Theo waited anxiously in the conference room with Lord Hain, waiting for Finnick and Jarreth to arrive. Theo had just heard word from one of the soldiers that the two lieutenants had arrived a short time ago, and they needed to speak to him as soon as possible. So, Theo sat in the conference room and waited, feeling uneasy with the rumours that were circulating around the kingdom. A servant came in with some refreshments and food and placed them on the table before leaving. Lord Hain reached over and took a glass of water for himself, then he offered one to Theo as well.

"Thank you, Lord Hain," Theo said, taking the glass.

A knock sounded at the door, then Finnick and Jarreth entered the room and sat down.

"Father," Finnick acknowledged.

"Son, it's good to see you're safe and unharmed," Lord Hain said plainly.

"Advisor Theo," Finnick nodded.

"Refreshments if you're hungry. I know you have just arrived back, so I asked someone to bring food for you," Theo said, gesturing to the plates in front of them.

"Thanks," Finnick said, as him and Jarreth helped themselves to the food and refreshments that were provided. Then they turned their attention to the two men sitting across from them.

"How is the King?" Lord Hain queried.

"King Nikolai is good. Captain Oberon is with him as he trains with Alvina to control the Crystal Gem," Finnick explained.

"Alvina?" Lord Hain questioned.

"The leader of the alicorn race," Finnick answered.

"So, the Crystal Gem exits," Theo said bewildered.

"Yes, there were a few obstacles along the way, but we managed to get it as a team," Finnick answered.

"The alicorn race exists," Lord Hain repeated to his son.

"Yes father, but they are hidden from the outside world for good reason," Finnick said straightforwardly.

Finnick knew what his father was thinking, and it wasn't good. He had prewarned Jarreth about not revealing the location to his father for good reason. Jarreth completely agreed.

"Of course, but if they were needed again in the future," Lord Hain said greedily, "where would one find them?"

"I'm not revealing the location father," Finnick said sternly.

"Of course," Lord Hain said backing off, angry at his son for the little confrontation.

Finnick knew his father wouldn't stop pestering him about the location after the meeting, and he was dreading the conversation. In the past, Lord Hain had proven to get greedy, and it always ended badly with either Finnick, or the house servants he grew up with.

"How is Queen Juliet?" Theo inquired, ignoring Lord Hain's

anger.

"The Queen has gone back to her home kingdom to inform her mother and Captain Issac of the coming war. Princess Iris and Prince Omari have done the same. Princess Iris is keeping an eye on the Prince of Darkness's movement with her animal abilities. We are to meet everyone near the cave in three days," Finnick explained. "If the Dark One moves earlier, Princess Iris will let us know."

"So King Nikolai is training with the Gem. How far has he reached?" Theo questioned.

"Just before we left, he managed to activate the Gem for five minutes before exhaustion hit him," Finnick replied.

"So, he has a long way to go," Lord Hain groaned. "Maybe he should give someone else a go at controlling the Gem. Maybe they'll get better results."

"Watch what you say next father, he is the King," Finnick warned.

Lord Hain and Finnick stared intently at each other for a few minutes before Lord Hain looked away angrily.

"Plus," Finnick said, looking to Theo, "King Nikolai is the only one who can use it."

"What do you mean?" Theo inquired.

"Just before we found the Gem, the riddle said, "The one who takes the bling, must be crowned a king, the one who is not, will most surely rot," Finnick said, looking to his father as he said the last part.

There was silence as Theo thought through what the lieutenants had just told him. King Nikolai wouldn't rest until he could control the Gem. Growing up with Nikolai, Theo had learned that he would put others first and himself last. He was confident that his friend would find a way to control the Gem for the sake of the world. However, worry etched in Theo's mind.

With Nikolai constantly thinking of other's first, he would forget to or deliberately put himself last. But Theo was glad that his friend had Juliet, as she knew the real Nikolai and was always looking after him. Theo looked up at the men around the table and sighed.

"Lord Hain, I need you to prepare your soldiers for war," Theo advised.

"Of course," Lord Hain said, standing up and leaving the room.

"What would you like us to do?" Finnick asked.

"Keep an eye on your father. Like you, I don't trust him. I'll talk to my brother about weapons," Theo revealed. "But I suggest you sharpen your skills."

"Of course," Finnick said.

Jarreth nodded then walked out with Finnick.

Theo sat and thought about the meeting with Lord Hain. His reputation was true, according to what Nikolai, Fitzwilliam and Finnick had told him. He would have to be careful with him until Nikolai and Juliet came back.

He sighed to himself. He was exhausted, but he got up and went to visit his brother.

◆ ◆ ◆ ◆ ◆

As Finnick and Jarreth walked back to the soldier's barracks, Finnick was glad that Theo was put in charge of the kingdom while the King and Queen were away, instead of his father. He was also glad that Theo was prewarned about how his father can be at times. As Finnick and Jarreth entered the barracks, they saw Finnick's father leaning against the wall sharpening his knife, not acknowledging their presence. Finnick and Jarreth walked past him without a word.

"Finnick, a word," Lord Hain said not looking up.

Finnick sighed to himself. This was not going to be a pleasant conversation. He nodded to Jarreth, who went on ahead, allowing the father and son to talk. But Finnick knew that Jarreth would be close by and hidden. Walking over to his father Finnick braced for the conversation.

"Yes father," Finnick answered.

"Next time you threaten me in front of others, I will make your life miserable. Or shall I show you how angry I am with one of the household staff you call friend," Lord Hain threatened.

Finnick swallowed the lump in his throat and answered his father. "Won't happen again, sir."

"No, it won't. Next time it happens, you can be certain it will not end well for your friends," Lord Hain said, standing inches away from Finnick. "Understood."

"Yes, sir," Finnick uttered.

Lord Hain walked away and left Finnick standing in anger and fear. From behind, Jarreth came over to check on him after the confrontation, knowing how Finnick felt about his father.

"*Are you okay?*" Jarreth asked.

"Yup," Finnick lied.

Jarreth looked at his friend with an eyebrow raised.

"No. I really dislike my father, and I fear for the household servants that have to put up with him," Finnick confessed.

"*At least they know you'll never be like him,*" Jarreth signed.

"Yes, thankfully," Finnick said relaxing.

"*Then trust that they will look out for one another,*" Jarreth signed. "*Focus on the mission Theo gave us. Obviously, Theo doesn't trust your father. We just have to make sure your father doesn't do anything behind Theo's back.*"

"Yes, I wouldn't put it past my father to do something like that," Finnick expressed. "Okay, let's go."

✦ ✦ ✦ ✦ ✦

"I'm relieved that King Nikolai and the others have managed to find the Crystal Gem," Fitzwilliam said, clearly impressed.

"Yes, me too. But the way Lord Hain acted during the meeting. I don't trust him," Theo said worriedly.

"King Nikolai doesn't trust him either. Have you asked someone to keep an eye on him?" Fitzwilliam asked.

"Yes. Finnick and Jarreth," Theo said.

"Are you sure Finnick would be up to the job? It is his father he is watching out for," Fitzwilliam said, smashing the metal he just took out of the fire.

"Believe me, if you saw how Finnick supported the King against his father during the meeting, you would see he clearly doesn't like his father very much," Theo said impressively. "Plus, all the stories he told Nikolai and I when we grew up together, doesn't make him sound like a very good man, Lord or father."

"Well, alrighty then. They are the two best people for the job. After all Oberon did choose them both as Lieutenants," Fitzwilliam said, wiping the sweat from his forehead.

"Yes, I agree," Theo said nodding. "Well, I best head back to the palace. I have a lot to prepare before we head off to war."

"I'll keep making the weapons, and if I hear anything suspicious, I'll let you know," Fitzwilliam said, putting the metal back into the fire. "Stay safe brother."

"You too, Fitzwilliam, thanks," Theo said, walking out of the blacksmith shop.

CHAPTER TWENTY-ONE

"Some have in fact already turned away to follow Satan."

1 Timothy 5:15

Serpentina slithered her way around the forest floor near the cave of Akuma, trying to find the Gem that Claud had hidden from her. She really thought that Claud would reveal the location in order to live, but she wouldn't have let him live anyway. She wanted to be the only one the master needed and relied on. It had been that way at the beginning just like she wanted, but as more people joined his cause, she had gotten jealous and forgotten by her master. She made sure to change that, as she worked her way around the newcomers, ensuring they never returned from their missions. Serpentina knew that withholding information about the two lieutenants' strength and fighting abilities, would result in Harkin's demise. She knew Selina wouldn't complete her mission because she wasn't informed about how strong Issac was, and his experience and skills gained as a wanderer. She knew that Anna wouldn't survive the encounter with the Captain of Zolatta, as she was still new to her abilities, but Serpentina encouraged her anyways. She also knew Mildred couldn't handle the creatures of darkness. Part of her knew that Mildred would turn to the other side once things got too difficult. She was glad when she did, because the price of betrayal was death. Serpentina didn't feel the slightest bit of remorse or guilt for her actions. She loved being the centre of attention and loved being relied on. It made her feel needed and powerful.

Serpentina came to the edge of the forest and let out a frustrated sigh.

"Where is it?" she yelled.

She slithered back to where she came from deep within the forest and began her search again. As frustrated as she was, she wouldn't go back to the master without the Gem. Even if it meant she had to search the forest for days. Claud wouldn't have put it too far, so it had to be close enough to the entrance of the cave.

But where?

She spent all day yesterday searching for it with no results. She had to find it soon, otherwise the master would know something was up, and she didn't want to disappoint him. Especially since he was so close to his goal.

Serpentina slithered her way past the banyan tree that grew near the cave and stopped suddenly. Something glittered against the sun. She circled back and came closer to the tree. She could see the sun shining against something on the ground just near the roots of the tree.

Something small and shiny.

She smiled to herself and let out a small cheer. The master would be pleased with her. She began transforming back to human so she could have a closer look to see if it was the Gem. Once the change was complete, she bent down and picked up the small sapphire Gem. Holding it in her hands she smiled. Her master's goal was finally complete. After being trapped for thousands of years, he would finally get his revenge on the world. Serpentina made herself presentable before she ran back to the cave of Akuma, to show her master the Gem. Little did she realise she was being watched the entire time by an eagle, who took flight once Serpentina entered the cave, reporting back to its own master what it had just seen.

Once Serpentina was inside, she ignored the other followers and ran straight up to the Prince of Darkness, eager to show him the Gem.

"Master," Serpentina said, bowing before him.

"Where have you been? Where is Claud?" he barked.

"I didn't trust Claud, so I followed him. I found out that he was going to keep the Gem for himself. So, I intercepted him. Unfortunately, he wouldn't give it up without a fight. So, we fought, but after I defeated him, I retrieved the Gem to bring it back to you," Serpintina lied, as she held up the Gem.

The Prince of Darkness stared at the sapphire Gem, before taking it from Serpentina. He held it up for a closer look and smiled.

"Well done, Serpentina," the Prince of Darkness said, caressing her cheek.

Serpentina smiled at the master's touch.

"Bring me some water and a mortar and pestle," the Prince of Darkness ordered.

Serpentina jumped up and ran to the stone table in the corner of the cave. After moving other objects on the table that had been stolen by passersby, she found what she was looking for. She ran back to the master and placed the mortar and pestle and a flask of water in front of him. She watched as the Prince of Darkness placed the sapphire Gem into the mortar, then smashed it into tiny pieces using the pestle. The Prince of Darkness then took the water and filled up the mortar. Once the contents were mixed, he held it up to his mouth to drink. He drank the contents of the mortar until he had swallowed every last bit of the Gem. He wiped his mouth and smiled at his followers, then closed his eyes and sat down and waited till the Gems healing abilities took effect. Minutes passed by and he could feel the strength in his bones getting stronger by the minute. He looked at his hands as he clenched them into fists then flexed them out again. His strength was coming back. He slowly stood up and stretched out the rest of his body. He then began to laugh so loud it echoed throughout the cave.

"COME FORWARD MY CREATURES OF DARKNESS!" the Prince of Darkness yelled. "COME OUT OF THE SHADOWS IN WHICH YOU HIDE FROM."

One by one the creatures he had summoned slowly walked out of the shadows of the cave. The followers moved in unison and bowed before their master. The minotaur's grunted as they each held a giant axe in their hand. The cyclops held onto their clubs and roared ferociously. Werewolves howled in unison as the hell hounds growled with hunger. Serpentina watched in awe at the master and his creatures. She decided to join in, so she transformed into a Basilisk, hissing when the transformation was complete. She then glided to the front where her master stood smiling. From the front, the Prince of Darkness looked at the number of creatures he had summoned to help him take over the world. The kingdoms had no chance with his creatures and followers combined. Even if they all came together with their own army, he would still have more than enough creatures to take them down once and for all.

The last time his creatures made their presence, was when he was free to roam the earth thousands of years ago. But when he got trapped by the God of Light, so did his creatures. His creatures haven't been around for thousands of years. So, they were forgotten by men. Meaning he had an advantage. This generation of warriors had no idea how to fight his creatures of darkness.

He laughed to himself.

"This will be too easy," the Prince of Darkness told himself. Then fear kicked in as he remembered the Crystal Gem. His weakness. The Gem of light. Searching the crowd he eventually laid eyes on Serpentina.

"Serpentina," he called.

Serpentina slithered up to the Prince of Darkness and bowed her head.

"Yesssssss, Master," she hissed.

"What has become of Anna and her search for the Crystal Gem," he barked.

"She has not come back, Master," she replied.

"WHAT!!!!" he roared.

Serpentina slithered back from the master, so she was out of his way as he fumed over the fact that the Gem still had not been found.

"Maybe the King hasn't found the Crystal Gem, Master," Serpentina said, trying to calm him down.

The Prince of Darkness turned and faced Serpentina with hatred and anger. He raised his hand at her, but stopped himself before he let his rage out. He still needed her so he could complete his goal. So instead, he conjured up a dagger made of dark magic and pelted it at the nearest cyclops. It grunted in pain at the dagger sticking out of its neck, before collapsing to the ground and dying before its master.

Veda, a follower who could turn into a vulture, flew in and landed next to the Prince of Darkness.

"What news do you bring," the Prince of Darkness fumed.

"They have found the Crystal Gem," Veda squawked.

"WHAT!!!!" the Prince of Darkness roared.

Veda spread her wings and flew further back so she wouldn't

be another victim of her master's rage. She landed on the ground not far from her master and waited for instructions.

"That Crystal Gem is the only thing that can get in the way of my plans," the Prince of Darkness growled. "How did they manage to find it?"

"Malachi and Mildred gave the King and Queen of Zolatta an alicorn. That alicorn led them to the Crystal Gem's whereabouts," Veda explained.

The Prince of Darkness tried to control his anger, but the fact that Malachi had helped the King and Queen in finding the Crystal Gem made him more furious. The God of Light still had an influence in this world, but he was too preoccupied with his own plans that he forgot about the messenger and what he would bring.

"Malachi," the Prince of Darkness snarled. "Always getting in the way of my plans."

"What do you want me to do?" Veda asked.

"Maintain a watch from the skies and report their location to me," the Dark One commanded.

"Yes Master," Veda said, then flew out of the cave.

"And me, Master?" Serpentina asked.

"Focus on the Griffin, we still may be able to use him," the Prince of Darkness scowled. "Offer him gold, power, anything that he wants to get him on our side."

"As you wish, Master," Serpentina said smiling.

The Prince of Darkness turned back to his creatures of darkness and smiled at the crowd before him. The numbers were in his favour, so what if the King of Zolatta had the Crystal Gem in his possession. He could still win this war with the numbers on his side. The Prince of Darkness shouted for the attention of his followers and creatures. The cave went silent as they all turned their attention to him and waited to hear what he had to say.

"We go to war," the Prince of Darkness yelled to his army. "We will rule the land of men. Kill anyone who gets in our way."

The cave thundered with different roars and howls as the creatures celebrated the end of their days of hiding. The Prince of Darkness turned and walked out of the cave of Akuma. One by one the creatures followed him out into the world of man. Behind them, the followers trailed behind, eager to start the new world they had been promised. A promise of freedom and power.

Little did they know, it was all a trap. They were just disposable pawns of the Dark One.

After walking a mile, the Prince of Darkness stopped and breathed in the fresh air. After thousands of years being chained to the cave by the God of Light, he was finally free.

Free to cause fear, destruction, and war.

CHAPTER TWENTY-TWO

"Put on the whole armour of God, that you may be able to stand against the wiles of the devil. For we do not wrestle against flesh and blood, but against principalities, against powers, against the rulers of darkness in this age."

Ephesians 6

"Well done, young King. You are now ready to take on the Dark One," Alvina said, smiling at the progress.

Nikolai, hands on his knees, tried to control his breathing. He had been training non-stop since the others had left to prepare for the war, and he was exhausted from all the training. He had practiced all day, every day, using the Crystal Gem until he could activate it with ease. Finally, after days of training, the results had finally paid off.

"Congratulations Your Highness," Oberon said, giving him some water.

"Thanks Captain," Nikolai said, taking the offered water flask.

Nix ran up to Nikolai and barked once before running around playfully, before coming in close for a pat. Nikolai smiled as he watched Nix full of energy. After receiving a good pat Nix sat beside Nikolai as he rested from his training.

After a mouthful of water Nikolai turned to Alvina. "Thank you for all the training. I appreciate it."

"Defeating the Dark One affects us all. I will do what I can to help," she replied.

"Any news about the Prince of Darkness?" Nikolai asked.

Alvina and Oberon exchanged guilty glances. Then Oberon cleared his throat, unsure about how to respond.

"What is it?" Nikolai asked, suddenly fearful.

Oberon cleared his throat then spoke.

"One of Princess Iris's hawks came back a couple of hours ago with some news," Oberon explained. "The wolf who stole the Gem from Queen Julia, got into a fight with one of the other followers, but he hid the Gem before the encounter."

"Why would he do that?" Nikolai questioned, confused.

"They were most likely fighting for power or favour from the Prince of Darkness himself," Alvina guessed.

Nikolai quickly explained to Oberon what Alvina had just said, and he nodded in agreement.

"Makes sense," Oberon agreed. "Queen Juliet made the decision to move the army now, because it would only be a matter of time before the other follower found the Gem, and give it to the Prince of Darkness."

"Smart move," Nikolai said "So, where is the army now?"

"A couple of miles from the cave of Akuma, waiting for you," Oberon said.

"All of the kingdom's armies?" Nikolai asked.

"Yes, Your Highness, they all moved together," Oberon said. "They are just waiting for you."

Another alicorn neighed as it cantered up to Alvina. Alvina turned to listen to what it had to say. Nikolai and Oberon looked to each other in concern as the alicorns communicated in a hurry. Then Alvina spun to face Nikolai and Oberon and spoke quickly.

"Another hawk arrived. The Prince of Darkness has been revived. He's heading towards the King's army," she said, panicking. "We must go now. Terran and Azul will fly yourself and your Captain to the battlefield."

Alvina turned and called to both stallions. Terran, a chestnut brown stallion came cantering up to Alvina, then bowed in front of her. Azul, a black Stallion came up next to Terran and bowed to Alvina. Alvina relayed the information to both male alicorn's while Nikolia interpreted for Oberon.

Azul and Terran trotted up to King Nikolai and Captain Oberon and bowed before them.

"Azul and Terran will fly us there, while Alvina prepares the rest of her race. She will then meet us on the battlefield," Nikolai told Oberon, while attaching his sword to his belt.

Oberon chose Azul to ride and mounted the black alicorn awkwardly, while Nikolai mounted Terran with ease.

"Nix, follow Juliet's scent and protect her," Nikolai told the wolf.

Nix barked in acknowledgment than ran towards the exit, where one of the alicorn's had it open ready for them. Nikolai and Oberon followed. Once they exited the waterfall, the alicorn's built up their speed then took flight.

"Oh boy," Oberon said, hanging onto Azul's mane.

Azul neighed at Nikolai.

"Azul is asking if you're afraid of heights?" Nikolai asked Oberon.

"Not afraid, just not a huge fan," Oberon said, feeling nervous. Azul neighed again.

"Azul said he will try to make the flight as steady as he can, so just relax," Nikolai laughed.

"Uh, thanks, Azul," Oberon said, nervously.

Both alicorn's soared through the sky at top speed. The morning was turning to afternoon as they got closer to their destination. It was a clear and sunny day. Perfect conditions for a battle. But that still made Nikolai uneasy. In war your bound to lose people, and this war wasn't with human beings, it was with monsters.

"Your Highness," Oberon said, pointing towards the horizon.

Nikolai looked to where Oberon was pointing and saw smoke rising towards the sky. His heart pounded in his chest as he thought of Juliet. Looking down at the ground below, he could just make out Nix's small form running at top speed towards the destination of the smoke.

"God of Light, protect the people I care about please," Nikolai whispered fearfully.

✦ ✦ ✦ ✦ ✦

"Hold your position," Issac called to his men.

The men that stood behind the royals, were on edge and afraid as they saw the Prince of Darkness and his army coming closer. Black smoke surrounded the Prince of Darkness as he walked forward in confidence. With his creatures of darkness behind him and his followers walking alongside them, they looked terrifying. Juliet sat atop of Amisha, waiting patiently for her husband to arrive and lead the army. She prayed for strength and wisdom that he would be able to use the Gems abilities. Looking towards the incoming army Juliet felt scared and afraid for her people. She had read about the creatures that plagued the world thousands of years ago, and feared fighting them now. As she and her people made their way over to the battlefield hours before, she practiced using her emerald Gem as much as she could. She wanted to be able to help others during the fight, and not feel completely useless.

Wishing Nikolai was with her, she scanned the horizon again. To her disappointment there was still no sign. She smiled at the King and Queen of Neylon who looked her way. They were dressed in red royal battle clothes, and were presenting themselves as confident. They each sat on a horse with their army behind them ready for battle.

"Is this your first war, Queen Juliet?" Queen Nala asked.

"No, sadly it is not," Juliet replied. "How about you, Your Highness?"

"No. I was hoping we wouldn't have another in my lifetime," Queen Nala said sadly.

"I completely understand," Juliet said with sympathy.

Juliet turned to her right and saw her mother, Queen Julia, and King Issac. They were dressed in the royal blue battle armour, and held their weapons at ease. Issac had his army behind him waiting for their orders to fight. They both sat on their horses, close to one another, hand in hand, waiting for the right time to strike. Looking further down, Juliet saw Princess Iris and Queen Athena attired in purple battle clothes. The different types of animals that Iris managed to ask for help, stood behind her and her mother, waiting patiently for the command. Their own army stood beside the animals, weapons ready, waiting for the Queen's order. Juliet could see a variety of different animals on the battlefield such as gorillas, tigers, bears, hawks, eagles, and snakes, as they stood ready and waiting for orders from Princess Iris. Behind Juliet was her own army from the Kingdom of Zolatta, which was being led by the former Captain of the Royal Guard, Lord Hain, while Oberon was with Nikolai. Looking ahead Juliet tensed. The Prince of Darkness and his army were getting closer, and Nikolai and Oberon were still not here yet.

"Your Highness," Juliet heard Finnick from behind her.

Juliet turned and looked at Finnick, the first lieutenant.

"Yes, Lieutenant," Juliet questioned.

Finnick pointed to something in the distance that Juliet couldn't quite make out. Squinting her eyes against the sun's bright light, she saw two figures riding alicorn's heading towards them. Juliet's relief showed on her face as the other's looked in the direction she was looking. Nikolai and Oberon were arriving. Juliet felt relieved to know that her husband and Captain Oberon were okay. Turning back to the enemy Juliet stood her ground, ready for the command to strike.

Minutes later Nikolai and Oberon landed in front of everyone. He smiled and nodded at each royal that came as an ally, then spoke to the crowd before him.

"Today we fight for our freedom and for peace. We fight for our loved ones and our friends. We fight for our future. Today we fight as one kingdom, not four," Nikolai yelled to the armies.

A chorus of battle cries hollered in agreement, ringing throughout the battlefield. Everyone stood with their weapons raised, ready to fight for a free and peaceful future. Turning back around to face the Prince of Darkness, Nikolai stood ready to make the call.

Upon the hill, the Prince of Darkness stood and smiled at the scene before him. His followers and creatures snarled and snickered at the enemy before them. The Prince of Darkness ushered his followers and creatures into being quiet, then looked at Nikolai.

"Stand down and surrender, and I'll promise you'll all live," the Prince of Darkness yelled to everyone.

"Not a chance," Nikolai yelled back.

"KILL THEM ALL," the Prince of Darkness yelled.

Both creatures and followers ran down the hill and straight towards Nikolai's army.

"For our future," King Nikolai yelled to his army, raising his flaming sword.

"For our future," the soldiers cried out, weapons raised.

CHAPTER TWENTY-THREE

"You will hear of wars and rumours of wars but see to it that you are not alarmed. Such things must happen, but the end is still to come."

Matthew 24:6

"ATTACK," Iris yelled to her animal friends.

Seeing King Nikolai running ahead towards the Prince of Darkness with his sword raised, Iris called out to her animal friends to follow behind and attack the creatures of darkness, who were already running towards them.

The eagles and hawks took to the sky and flew straight down attacking the creatures with their sharp beaks and talons, causing them to bleed from open wounds and deep cuts. The brown bears that lived around the Kingdom of Kudzu ran forward with their teeth bared and their claws out. Coming upon a hell hound, one brown bear leaped upon the beast and sunk its teeth and claws into its neck, making it bleed out on the battlefield. Satisfied that the beast was dead the brown bear roared furiously then moved onto the next victim.

The tigers ran at top speed and intercepted the beasts that were heading towards the Princess of Kudzu. Jumping upon the werewolves, the tigers clawed and bit at the werewolf while wrestling with them for victory.

A group of pythons slithered their way into the battlefield before stopping in front of a werewolf. The group of pythons broke up and surrounded the wolf, hissing to one another in communication. One by one they lunged at the werewolf, taking turns biting the beast. Weakened from the pain and blood loss, the werewolf collapsed to the ground. Slithering up to the werewolf, a python opened its jaws wide enough to begin devouring its prey.

A band of gorillas ran forward and tackled a cyclops to the ground. They started pounding and beating the beast till it was no more. Once they were satisfied that the beast would not move again, the band of gorillas beat their chest and hooted in triumphant at their victory, before moving onto the next victim, a minotaur that was coming straight for them. Grunting to each other in communication, the band of gorillas surrounded the minotaur. The minotaur came at one of the gorillas with its axe, but the gorilla stopped the incoming weapon with its bare hands. The other gorillas surrounding the minotaur jumped up and snapped off its horn, plunging it into the beast's chest. Together the gorillas beat their chest and hooted at another victory.

"Nice going, Boris," Iris called out to one of the gorillas.

The gorilla hooted back at Iris, then went to join his brothers in battle.

After hearing a familiar sound, Iris turned and saw that the alicorn race had arrived, and were already joining in the battle. Relief filled her as she stood before Alvina, their leader.

"We have come to assist," Alvina said.

"Thank you," Iris said gratefully.

Alvina nodded then went to fight.

One of the alicorns used their horn to grow vines to bind a hell hound that was coming for them, while another alicorn used their horn to pierce the beast. Another used their horns power to move rocks and throw them at the enemy, while another used its wings to raise up a strong gust of wind.

Iris, taking on the abilities from her tiger friend Mala, ran onto the battlefield with her claws out, swiping at any creature that came close enough to her. Jumping up onto one of the cyclops she clawed at the creature's back. Dropping its club, the cyclops tried to grab Iris, but failed. It was now defenceless as it tried to shake off its persistent attacker. Jarreth came running up with his bow and arrow raised, then let the arrow fly straight into the cyclops heart. A loud thump rumbled the battlefield as the cyclops collapsed to the ground.

"Nice shooting," Iris said, coming up to kiss Jarreth on the cheek.

Jarreth smiled and quickly returned the kiss, then aimed his arrow towards his friend who was battling a hell hound. Releasing his bow, his arrow struck the side of the hell hound causing it to fall. Finnick used this opportunity to raise his giant axe, bringing it down onto the beast.

"Nice," Finnick said, giving his friend a thumbs up.

A loud roar got their attention and Jarreth, Iris and Finnick turned to see their next opponent. A minotaur. It growled at the three while clutching the axe in its hand. The three braced and readied their weapons for another attack. Finnick who was grinning to himself, turned, and looked at Jarreth with an idea forming in his mind.

"Why are you looking at me like that?" Jarreth signed to his friend.

"Like what?" Finnick said.

"That look you get when you have a crazy idea forming in that

big head of yours," Jarreth signed.

Finnick laughed. "It's where I store all my best ideas."

Jarreth smiled and shook his head as he laughed to himself.

"What crazy idea have you come up with this time?" Jarreth signed.

"I just thought you and Princess Iris could distract the beast for me, while I chop one of its horns off," Finnick said casually. "Easy, right."

Princess Iris looked at Finnick with her eyebrows raised. "You're joking right. That thing is huge."

The minotaur roared as it ran up to attack the three before they could finish planning their attack. The minotaur raised its axe and brought it down in the direction of Iris. Jarreth grabbed her out of the way, then began shooting his arrows at the beast continuously. As the beast was distracted with Jarreth, Iris snuck to the back of the minotaur and jumped up onto its back, using her claws to climb up to its shoulders. The minotaur began moving erratically trying to shake Iris off, but she held on firmly.

"Finnick, legs." Iris called out.

Finnick ran up to the minotaur and used his axe to slice its calves. Roaring in pain and anger the minotaur turned to Finnick but tripped, falling face first to the ground. Iris jumped off and backed away, as Finnick used his axe to slice off the horn, then used it to penetrate the beast's chest. The three stood before the dying beast, taking a minute to catch their breath.

"We need a holiday," Jarreth signed to the others.

"I agree," Finnick panted.

Iris laughed as she watched the two lieutenants, but her laughter turned silent when she noticed another beast creeping up towards them.

✦ ✦ ✦ ✦ ✦

On the other side of the battlefield, Omari came face to face with a follower of the Prince of Darkness.

Serpentina.

After seeing Nikolai run ahead into the battlefield, Omari begun his transformation into a griffin to help him fight in this war. At first, he was just fighting the creatures of darkness that the Dark One had summoned. But after a few victories, another much stronger opponent approached him. Serpentina circled him and admired how the gift turned out. Omari was appalled at her admiration about his griffin abilities. He grew up in isolation, had no friends, no freedom and even his parents feared him most days. It was no gift. It was a curse. A curse he wanted to get rid of, and defeating Serpentina was the key to his freedom.

He dug his talons into the ground to control his anger. Serpentina was in front of him, smiling at him, playing him. It was all a game to her. Omari thought he could end this battle quickly, but was proven wrong as he watched Serpentina's transformation.

A basilisk. A fearsome and deadly creature.

Omari quickly looked anywhere but her eyes and groaned inwardly. This battle wasn't going to be easy. A basilisk was a fearsome creature with strength and agility, and the ability to turn one to stone if you looked into its eyes.

"Handsome and smart," Serpentina praised, amazed that Omari knew not to gaze into her eyes.

"I've had plenty of time to study after you cursed me," Omari growled.

"Come now Prince, the Master has given you an amazing gift. A gift he can teach you how to control, if only you ask him," Serpentina explained.

"This is no gift. This is a curse," Omari said angrily.

"But it is a gift," Serpintina said smiling. "If you knew how to control it, you wouldn't think it was a curse."

Omari looked at his claws, then looked at his wings. He did enjoy flying, and it did give him certain useful abilities. But he was still classified as a freak to his bullies, and a burden to his parents. There was no hope for him to have a normal life. But the new friends he had made while on this journey, had accepted him as he was. Curse or no curse.

"Come join us and I can promise you the Master will show you how amazing you are," Serpentina coaxed.

"No," Omari stated.

"Your so-called friends are trying to take away your amazing abilities, when they should be accepting you as you are," Serpentina said, trying to discouraging him.

"They're not taking away my abilities. They're helping me be normal, and they do accept me," Omari said.

"Do they though?" Serpentina said, putting doubt in his mind.

Omari thought to himself for a moment, feeding the doubt in his mind.

"Do they?" Omari thought to himself.

Serpentina smirked to herself as she watched Omari ponder her words. Obviously, he was still experiencing doubt after being in isolation for so long. That's what she needed to do, keep him second guessing everyone and everything. Slithering her way to the side of Omari, she kept a look out to see if he would notice.

He was too distracted by his thoughts of doubt, so Serpentina lunged at Omari from behind. Omari turned at the last minute with his eyes closed and bit down on Serpentina's basilisk body. Screaming and hissing in pain Serpintina tried to slither away from Omari's hold, but Omari had her tightly within his jaws and talons. Serpentina bit Omaris's leg, forcing him to release his hold on her. She hissed at him and slithered away to a safe distance and watched him.

"How?" she asked him.

"What," Omari said smiling at her. "You took the time to curse me, but didn't take the time to learn my abilities."

"How dare you?" Serpentina fumed.

Omari with his eyes still closed, smiled at hearing her frustration.

Serpentina hissed again, baring her sharp teeth, and lunged forward towards Omari who dodged at the last minute. Omari used this close contact opportunity again and clawed at her. She slithered away, then lunged back quickly to strike at Omari again. Omari, barely escaping the previous encounter, fell to the ground as Serpentina brought her tail under Omari. Landing on his back Omari covered his eyes with his wings, and fought with his talons at Serpentina's incoming attack.

"Your hearing isn't so good now is it," she hissed venomously.

Omari just noticed the background noise, and what Serpentina was doing. She was leading him closer and closer to the main battlefield, causing his hearing to become difficult as he heard the enemy and ally's fight.

"You did do your research," Omari said, clutching his bleeding arm.

She smiled at him.

"I had a lot of free time while my Master was bound by the God of Light," she smiled. "Thousands of years."

She attacked him again. "To learn about humanity. To learn their weaknesses."

Omari swiped back at her, striking her in the face. Serpentina moved away and felt the wound and blood dripping from her face.

"What?" Omari questioned. "Thousands of years."

Serpentina began to laugh, despite the pain in her face.

"How old are you?" Omari asked with disgust.

"You know, if you ever hope to find a woman, you must never ask her age," she pouted. "It's insulting."

Omari waited, listening to Serpentina's movement.

"But you're right," she told him. "My Master needed someone by his side always, and I was there for him, never leaving his side. So, he gave me some of his powers to help me live through the ages. Watching, learning, listening, and teaching the world about how good my Master is."

"The Prince of Darkness is evil. He uses dark magic, and is manipulative. He tortures people, and he spreads hate and fear," Omari yelled in frustration.

"Don't you just love it," Serpentina said laughing.

Omari listened to hear where Serpentina was, then lunged in that direction while she was distracted with praising the Prince of Darkness. Once he had her snake body within his talons, he bit down again on her tail, making her bleed even more. She screamed in agony as she tried to shake him off, but she couldn't, as he held onto her firmly, not letting her go. After a few minutes of struggle, Serpentina began to weaken at the blood loss Omari had caused, along with all the other wounds she had. Eventually she collapsed to the ground panting and coughing up blood. Serpentina looked around trying to find her master. Once she saw him, she called out to him with tears in her eyes.

"Master. Help," she said coughing up more blood.

She didn't want to die, not yet, she wasn't ready. She was stupid enough to let her guard down with the griffin while praising her master. The Prince of Darkness looked towards Serpentina casually from the rock he sat on, while observing the battlefield, then looked away from her. Pain and rejection hit Serpentina, as she cried at her master's emotionless face towards her. She had given her life to him, and now he was just leaving her to die. Alone.

Eventually after losing too much blood, Serpentina took her last breath as she stared at her master for the last time. Omari stood by listening to Serpentina. When he heard her final breath leave her, he opened his eyes and looked around. He was still a good distance away from the battlefield. When he looked back at Serpentina's lifeless body, her basilisk form was in a horrendous state. Her body was covered in deep lacerations, bite marks and open wounds, that gushed out blood onto the ground. Suddenly Omari found himself covered in a bright light. He looked down at himself as he began to turn back into his human self. Once the transformation was complete, he felt someone wrap him with a jacket.

His mother stood beside him with some spare clothes in hand.

"I am so proud of you," she praised, smiling at her son.

"Thanks mom," Omari replied, taking the clothes to change.

Queen Nala stood up and turned to the battlefield with her fits raised, protecting her son from any incoming attack while he dressed.

CHAPTER TWENTY-FOUR

*"Put on the full armour of God,
so that you can take your stand against the devil's schemes."*

Ephesians 6:11

Juliet used her emerald Gem abilities to command the vines to bind the hell hounds, while Oberon took them down with his sword one by one. After taking care of the last hell hound, Oberon turned and focused on another incoming threat. Giant spiders scuttled along the battlefield as they made their way over to Oberon. The spiders had no remorse for the creatures it killed along the way, piercing them with its long sharp legs, as they got closer to Oberon and Juliet.

"I thought we got rid of all of Jorogumo's minions?" Juliet asked shocked.

"I wouldn't put it past the Prince of Darkness to have tricks up his sleeves," Oberon said, sword ready.

A massive spider ran towards Oberon and Juliet while shooting its webs at them both, repeatedly. Dodging the incoming attack, Oberon ran up to face the spider while Juliet helped keep the webs at bay with her vines. The creatures that were in their field of vison weren't so lucky. Any enemy that was unlucky to have been captured by the web was left behind. Desperately wanting to end this battle, Juliet used her vines to hold the spider's leg firmly on the ground. Unable to move, the spider began screeching loudly. But was silenced quickly by Oberon and his sword.

"I hope we don't have to deal with another spider," Juliet said with disgust.

"Me too, Your Highness," Oberon said looking at the dead spider. "Me too."

"Queen Juliet," Lord Hain called from behind her.

Juliet looked around to find Lord Hain running up towards her.

"What's wrong?" Juliet asked.

"Queen Julia requires your assistance in the medical tent," Lord Hain told her.

"Okay," Juliet said, looking around for her alicorn.

"Your Highness," Oberon said pointing ahead.

Juliet turned to find Amisha and Nix confronted by another spider. Thankfully, this one was smaller than what she and Oberon had just battled. Oberon ran ahead and intercepted the spider before it attacked again, killing it in a single blow. Nix barked his approval then turned and growled at the new threat coming from behind Juliet. Looking at the worried faces, Juliet turned to find another minotaur running towards them all.

"Go to Amisha and help your mother," Oberon said, running with Juliet and helping her mount Amisha. "Let Lord Hain and I deal with this. GO!"

Amisha galloped away from the incoming minotaur and headed away from the battlefield. Nix barked and ran from behind, attacking any creature that got to close to Juliet. At the edge of the battlefield, just before the medical tents stood, were a horde of creatures coming to prey on the weak and injured. Juliet got off her alicorn and acted fast before the medical tent was hit. Placing her hands on the ground, Juliet focused on the earth that was beneath her fingers. The earth Gem, which was now a ring on her finger, glowed. Suddenly the ground began to shake as something came up through the dirt. Bamboo stalks emerged from the ground and pierced any creatures that got to close to the tent. The soldiers that were protecting the medical tent ran ahead and finished off the creatures that were still alive, even after being caught and trapped by the bamboo stalks. Juliet looked up and was relieved to see she wasn't too late. Standing up, she saw the impact her bamboo stalks had done, grateful that her mother and the other volunteers in the medical tent were safe again.

"Congratulations Juliet, your earth powers have grown," Amisha said standing beside her in awe.

"Thanks Amisha," Juliet said, looking at her ring.

Once there was a clear path, Juliet and Amisha ran over to the entrance as the soldiers continued to clean up outside.

"Thanks, Your Highness," a soldier said as Juliet ran past.

"You're welcome," Juliet replied.

"I'll stay and help outside," Amisha told Juliet.

"Thank you, call if you need anything," Juliet said.

"Will do," Amisha neighed, then went to help the soldiers.

Once Juliet was inside the medical tent, she scanned the large room to find her mother. She was rushing around the room giving orders to the women who had volunteered to help during the war. As soon as she saw Juliet she stopped and smiled, relief showing on her face.

"Mother what can I do?" Juliet asked.

"Beds one through to five, please," Queen Julia replied gracefully.

"Okay," Juliet said heading over to the beds.

Queen Julia smiled then went back to her duties as the wounded kept coming in.

Juliet ran to the first bed and knelt towards the wounded soldier. He was out cold from his open wound. Assessing the severity, Juliet made the decision to heal him as his wound ran from his knee to his ankle. After healing him for several long minutes she looked down to check his wound again. It was fully healed but the soldier was still unconscious. Checking his forehead, Juliet became concerned as he showed signs of a high temperature. The soldier was burning up, despite the afternoon chill outside. She quickly went over to the herb station and began collecting herbs that acted as a natural antibiotic. She took out the mortar and pestle and began crushing up the garlic, then she added honey and began to stir it into a paste.

"Anything I can do to help, Your Highness?" a volunteer asked.

"Oh, yes. Perfect timing. The patient in bed one needs this antibiotic. Can you help him drink this?" Juliet asked, giving the garlic and honey mixture to the volunteer.

"Of course," the volunteer said, taking the mixture.

After washing and drying her hands Juliet looked around the room, deJa'vu hitting her big time. Memories played through her mind, as she thought back to the war that plagued her kingdom for a while. She treasured the peace while it lasted, hoping she wouldn't have to go through another war in her lifetime. She sighed to herself, put the towel back on its hanger, and walked over to her next patient.

"Queen Juliet," a familiar voice said.

Juliet looked up to see first lieutenant Shaw staring back at her on the second bed.

"Riley," Juliet said, smiling at the familiar face.

"It's good to see you, Your Highness," she replied.

"You too, although I wish is was under better circumstances,"

Juliet said assessing her wounded arm.

"Me too, but I will happily fight for my Queen and Princess," Riley said. "And future King I hear."

"Yes, you heard right," Juliet said, as she started healing Riley's arm.

"How do you feel about it?" Riley whispered, looking around.

"About time, I say," Juliet chuckled. "I never knew my father, and Issac was always there, so I'm happy."

"I'm glad you're happy," Riley said, looking down at her arm. "How bad is it?"

"After I finish healing, you'll walk away with just a scar," Juliet reassured, as she continued to heal.

"That's good. I still have some fight in me and I'm eager to get back out there," Riley said.

"Don't worry, I'll have you out of here in no time," Juliet said, assessing Riley's arm.

Once Juliet was satisfied that there was no infection, and Riley's arm was fully healed, she let the lieutenant go as she had a lineup of patients waiting for her. But not before she wished good luck to her friend on the battlefield. As Juliet made her way over to bed number three, she suddenly stopped and looked around as a high-pitched scream rung out, inside the medical tent. She searched around for the danger until she found the culprit. A medium size spider was attached to one of the patient's chest as they lay unconscious, likely by the poison that the spider held. Queen Julia and some volunteers walked cautiously over to see how they could help the victim. They jumped back as the spider moved an inch on its victim, holding them even tighter, which scared the people inside the tent.

"I hate spiders," one volunteer said shivering.

"I don't mind them when they're small, but this is another thing entirely," another said in disgust.

"Be careful," Juliet warned. "They're poisonous."

Juliet walked over cautiously to the victim and spider, assessing the damage, and thinking of ways to extract the spider without hurting the person underneath.

"Any ideas?" Queen Julia asked.

"None," Juliet said worriedly.

She brought up her vines slowly and carefully, making sure the spider didn't see them from below. When the vines got to the height of the bed, she stopped and thought about how to progress further. Worry etched her face as she thought about the poison spreading further throughout the victim's body. From the corner of her eye Juliet saw her mother telling the soldiers who had come in to help, to stand down for the time being. They watched in fear as Juliet tried to think of a plan quickly. She had to act now otherwise she would lose the patient. She brought up her vines so quickly that the spider didn't realise what was happening until it was too late. Her vines wrapped around its many legs and torso, preventing it from harming the victim any further. As Juliet held it mid-air with her vines, it began to squirm and screech, moving erratically as it wanted to escape and feed. Juliet used her other hand to conjure up a plant, this one being bigger than the spider itself. The Venus Flytrap, well known for eating insects. Once the Venus Flytrap was fully rooted, it opened its long wide leaf blades and readied its trap for its prey. Juliet moved the spider over to the Venus Flytrap and dropped it into the plants open mouth. The leaf blades snapped shut as soon as the spider fell inside. The onlookers watched in awe and disgust as the plant tightened its grip on the spider as it ate, and eventually digested the spider.

"Smart thinking, Queen Juliet," a volunteer voiced.

"Thanks," Juliet said.

She walked over to the unconscious patient and looked up at her mother.

"How bad is it?" she asked.

"With both of us working together, they'll live," Queen Julia said. "Nice move with the plant."

"Thanks, I'll move it when it finishes digesting," Juliet said, looking back at the plant.

"No need. We may need to use it again," Queen Julia said.

Turning back to the patient in front of her, Juliet began to follow her mother's direction on how to save the life that lay on the bed in front of her, and not to worry about what was digesting behind her.

CHAPTER TWENTY-FIVE

*"With the belt of truth buckled around your waist, with the
breastplate of righteousness in place, and with your feet fitted
with the readiness that comes from the gospel of peace.
Take up the shield of faith, with which you can extinguish
all the flaming arrows of the evil one. Take the helmet of salvation
and the sword of the Spirit, which is the word of God."*

Ephesians 6:14-17

Queen Nala fought back-to-back with her husband and son while
surrounded by a horde of hell hounds. As each one came within
distance, she punched them with enough force that their bones
broke. Each creature that was hit by Queen Nala, King Jabari or
Prince Omari, would collapse onto the ground unable to withstand
the mighty force. Unable to move from their broken bones, the
hell hounds were no match for this mighty strong family.

"Nice one, my dear," King Jabari shouted.

"Thanks dear, to your left," Queen Nala yelled.

King Jabari turned to his left and saw the creature his wife
had warned him about. He brought his sword down onto the hell

hound with enough force that it was killed instantly.

"Son, how's your side?" King Jabari asked.

"All good on my side," Omari said, punching each beast that came within distance to his family.

Omari stood with his fists ready for the next attack, only it didn't come. He looked around and saw all the dead hell hounds across the battlefield in front of them. A smile formed on his face for the little victory they had.

"Who's the strongest family here," King Jabari shouted in triumphant.

"We are," Omari laughed along with his father.

King Jabari and Omari laughed and hugged one other, while Queen Nala stood back and smiled to herself. Her family was back together now. King Jabari and Omari broke their hug as they heard something behind them. Bracing for another attack they stood ready, but were met with a horrible scene before them. Queen Nala had been grabbed by a cyclops. But instead of being terrified, Queen Nala began attacking the cyclops while still within its grasp. King Jabari and Prince Omari didn't hesitate and started attacking the beast.

"Let go of my wife," King Jabari yelled, slicing the beast's calves.

The cyclops roared furiously at them, then threw Queen Nala to the ground before running up towards its newest victim.

"Mother," Omari cried out.

"Go to her Omari. I'll deal with this," King Jabari said.

Omari, panicking for his mother's wellbeing, ran over and skidded to a stop beside her. He gently lifted her head so she could see him, while brushing her hair away from her face. Blood oozed from open wounds and Omari tried his best to stop the bleeding.

"Mother," Omari cried.

"My son," she whispered.

"I'm sorry," Omari cried.

"It's not your fault," Queen Nala assured, wiping the tears from Omari's face.

Omari looked around the battlefield and saw his father was still battling the cyclops. He looked towards Nikolai in the distance but couldn't see Queen Juliet with him. She had to be in the medical tent. He had to get his mother there; only then will Juliet be able to save her. Omari scooped his mother up and held her firmly, then ran to the back of the battlefield where the medical tent stood surrounded by an army of guards.

"Hold on mother," Omari told her as he ran.

King Jabari focused his attention on the cyclops, but from the corner of his eyes, he could see his son running towards the medical tent with the injured Queen Nala. Praying that his wife was okay, he turned back to the beast in front of him.

"Let's make this quick," King Jabari sneered.

The cyclops threw its axe at King Jabari, but he dodged it at the last minute, as he skidded to the ground. Quickly getting back up King Jabari ran up to the cyclops and slashed its ankles from behind. The cyclops stumbled then righted itself, turning toward its enemy. King Jabari ran up again and stabbed the cyclops in the leg multiple times before backing away from its angry outburst. Picking up the club again, the cyclops ran up to King Jabari and swung his club at him. King Jabari ducked low to the ground to avoid being hit, then ran up and stabbed the cyclops in the leg again, before backing away from its outburst and rage. The cyclops struggled to walk ahead, feeling dizzy from the blood loss. It took another slow step towards King Jabari letting out a loud roar as it took another step closer. King Jabari came in close using a great amount of force, and sliced the cyclops in the knee. The cyclops stumbled and fell to the ground. King Jabari quickly ran around to face the beast head on. He then lifted his sword up and brought it down onto the cyclops without remorse.

"For my wife," he whispered.

After making sure the creature was dead, King Jabari ran to the medical tent hoping he wasn't too late. Upon opening the tent door, he stopped and stared at the scene before him. Volunteers and medical staff rushed around inside trying to heal and help the injured. His eyes crossed the room until he found his son watching from a distance as Queen Julia and Queen Juliet healed his wife. He walked over to Omari and watched his wife as she was being healed, praying to the God of Light that he wouldn't take her yet.

"How's Nala," he whispered to Omari.

"Broken arm, broken ribs and a few open wounds," Omari told his father. "Other than that, she will be okay."

King Jabari left out a breath of relief.

"I'm sorry," Omari said, beginning to cry.

"Why, you did nothing wrong?" he said to his son, confused.

"I got distracted. We're in the middle of a war. We should be on guard all the time. I'm sorry," Omari said wiping his eyes.

"Not your fault son. We were celebrating a small victory," King Jabiri said, hugging his son.

King Nikolai caught up with Lord Hain and Captain Oberon on the battlefield and looked around. Dead soldiers, animals, followers, and creatures lay scattered on the battlefield. The smell of blood and decaying bodies lingered in the air. The soldiers and animals who were still alive, slowly made their way back to the medical tent to get their wounds healed and get some rest. The creatures and followers who were still alive, scurried back to their master who sat patiently on the hill.

"Looks like they're retreating for the time being," Oberon said looking around the battlefield. "But why?"

"Heavy losses on their side," Nikolai guessed. "I came across a few of his followers. They were strong, but relied on defensive strategies. And they weren't experienced."

"Guess they didn't get the memo," Oberon said.

"The memo?" Nikolai asked.

"With great power comes great responsibility," Oberon laughed.

Nikolai laughed along with his Captain.

"All jokes aside. I'm being serious. What if they couldn't handle the power," Oberon said.

"Why accept it in the first place then?" Nikolai asked, confused.

"With Juliet and her powers, she trained. She went from knowing nothing to being strong. What if the followers thought having power was good and all, but didn't train to get any better," Oberon said, letting the question hang.

"They would know the bare minimum to defend themselves, and the thought of having power would make them unstoppable to the weak, but weak to the strong," Nikolai said nodding in agreement.

"Some of these followers are just talk, but others aren't. We must be careful," Oberon advised.

"Agreed," Nikolai replied.

Finnick, Jarreth and Princess Iris ran up to Oberon and Nikolai. Once they all caught their breaths, Finnick finally spoke.

"Something's going on up there," Finnick said, pointing to where the Prince of Darkness sat.

"What is it?" Oberon asked.

Finnick gestured to Princess Iris, and she stepped forward to reveal the information she had just gotten.

"One of my animal friends have just informed me that the

Prince of Darkness is weak and vulnerable at the moment. He's been summoning more creatures after the first wave," Iris explained. "And these creatures are more fierce and deadly."

"Makes sense as to why his followers have surrounded him," Oberon said, observing.

"I agree. I think it's safe to assume that the ones who are protecting him, are the ones to be careful of," Nikolai said.

"Also, the Prince of Darkness has underestimated us and our strength in fighting together," Oberon said.

"I agree. It's a relief. Let's get the wounded to the medical tent while we have the time," Nikolai ordered his soldiers. "And pray for some rest."

"Yes, Your Highness," Lord Hain and Captain Oberon said, as they ran off with the lieutenants and Princess Iris following behind.

Nikolai looked back over to the Prince of Darkness, who was sitting on a hill in the distance. He was shocked to see the Dark One so weak and vulnerable. He was frustrated that he couldn't do anything, as all the creatures and followers were surrounding their master, protecting him while he regained his strength.

"Nikolai," Juliet called, coming up to him.

Nikolai turned around and smiled at his wife. Holding out his hand to her, she took it, and they embraced one another, treasuring the moment.

"How are you?" Juliet asked.

"As good as you can feel being in the middle of war," Nikolai said.

"What's bothering you?" Juliet said, looking up while still in the embrace of her husband.

"The Prince of Darkness. He's weak and vulnerable now, but he's surrounded by his followers," Nikolai said looking down at her. "I wish there was some way we could sneak around his creatures and followers, and get to him while he's in that state."

"Me too. We've already lost so many people, I don't want to lose anymore," Juliet said sadly.

"Let's enjoy the peace while it lasts," Nikolai said, caressing her face then kissing her forehead.

"Your Highnesses," someone cleared their throat from behind them.

Nikolai and Juliet turned to find Captain Chase and Lieutenant Riley standing behind them. They both bowed, before Chase spoke again.

"Get some rest. We'll keep watch and let you know when the Prince of Darkness makes a move," Chase said.

"Are you sure?" Juliet asked.

"Yes, I'm sure," Chase replied, nodding.

"Go and get some rest Queen Juliet. You've being healing nonstop since the war started," Riley urged.

"Okay," Juliet sighed in defeat. "Thank you both."

"Thank you," Nikolai said.

Taking Juliet's hand, Nikolai walked over to the back of the camp where Amisha lay by the fire, resting. While walking past the soldiers, he saw some who were lucky to be alive, and others who were mourning for their fallen friends in the first wave. Juliet squeezed his hand in comfort and smiled at him. He smiled back and held her closely. Amisha's ears twitched as she heard movement close by, and she lifted her head to see what was interrupting her nap. She neighed happily at the sight of Juliet and Nikolai. Other alicorn's who were resting nearby had raised their heads at the noise. When they realised it wasn't a threat, they lay their heads down and rested while they had the chance.

"Amisha how are you?" Juliet asked, offering her a carrot.

"Exhausted, but good," Amisha replied, scooping up the carrot into her mouth.

"Where's Alvina?" Nikolai asked, looking around.

"She sustained some injuries, and is currently being healed by Queen Julia," Amisha said, sniffing for more carrots.

"Oh," Juliet and Nikolai said, looking at each other with concern.

"Don't worry, she's fine. We knew what we signed up for when we offered to help in the war," Amisha encouraged.

"Thanks Amisha," Juliet said, patting her head and giving her another carrot.

Juliet and Nikolai sat close to Amisha, relishing the warmth from the fire. Nix came up and rested near Nikolai and Juliet's feet, falling asleep almost instantly after the first attack and protecting Juliet. The sounds of quiet chatter drifted amongst the campsite while others still talked about the first wave. The evening chill turned into a cold night as the hours went by, making the soldiers tend to the fire more often to savour the warmth. Juliet's head relaxed on Nikolai's shoulder as she fell into a peaceful sleep. Nikolai smiled as he wrapped his arms around her and brought her closer to him. His eyes were drifting as he looked around. He rubbed them with his fingers as he fought to stay awake. Sensing his struggle, Amisha spoke up.

"King Nikolai, rest. We have soldiers, animals and alicorn's taking in turns for guard duty," Amisha whispered.

"I-," Nikolai began, but yawned instead.

"Rest before our next attack. You won't be any good to us falling asleep on the battlefield. We need you ready and awake for the next wave," Amisha said, urging the King to listen.

"Okay," Nikolai said yawning. "But first sign of movement you wake me. Please."

"Of course," Amisha agreed.

Nikolai yawned again and looked back to where the Prince of Darkness sat. His many followers were still surrounding him, protecting him from any surprise attacks. He saw many Komodo Dragons that stood their ground, protecting their master. It was no wonder they hadn't seen them up until now, or had they just been summoned recently. Either way, they were the perfect defence while the Dark One regained his strength.

Seems like the Prince of Darkness isn't all that powerful, Nikolai thought, drifting off to sleep.

CHAPTER TWENTY-SIX

"When Joshua heard the noise of the people shouting,
he said to Moses, 'There is the sound of war in the camp.'"

Exodus 32:17

Draykon stood in front of his master, protecting him from the enemy that stood below at the bottom of the hill. He could see light coming from below, so he assumed the enemy was taking this time to prepare for the second wave. He dug his claws into the dirt in frustration. After his master had used up most of his powers to summon more creatures, he was weak. His master had asked him to use his gift now, so Draykon had taken the opportunity to transform into a Komodo Dragon. When he was in this form, he felt powerful. The gift for following the master had proven to be worth his time, but Draykon craved more. He had thought about double crossing his master, but thought it wasn't the right time. There were to many followers still alive, and not many chances he would get out alive.

"Draykon," the Prince of Darkness rasped.

"Yesssssss, Master," Draykon hissed, bowing before his

master.

"Use your gift I gave you to infiltrate the camp, and kill the King that holds the Crystal Gem," the Prince of Darkness ordered.

"Yes, Master," Draykon said, bowing before he left.

Running swiftly down the hill, Draykon kept an eye and ear out for the enemy nearby. He came to a stop at the bottom of the hill and scanned the terrain. He had to be careful because King Nikolai had the Princess of Kudzu as an ally, and she had the power to communicate with animals. That was a big issue for him as he was planning to sneak in undetected, but that didn't stop him. His master had given him a gift so powerful that he felt unstoppable. The gift to turn into a Komodo Dragon. The Komodo Dragon is the largest living lizard species on the planet, which made Draykon all the more terrifying. Once he was fully healed, he trained every day to become the strongest out of the other followers. In his Komodo Dragon form, Draykon was three metres in length, courtesy from the Prince of Darkness who needed him to be unbeatable. As Draykon tested his new abilities and strengths, he found that as the dragon he could run fast enough to attack and kill a human, which is what he wanted. He also learnt from experience that he had a venomous bite, which delivered a toxin that could cause infections, which can lead to death if not treated straight away. His dragon tail was longer than his scaly body, and he could use it for support when he stood up on his hind legs. Perfect for an incoming attack by his enemies, and making him have the upper hand in battle by having both an attack and defence system. The one thing that made Draykon hard to kill was his armoured scales that covered his body. The only way to kill him would be to attack at his most vulnerable spots, being his eyes, nose, and mouth.

Being careful not to be seen by the enemy, Draykon peaked through the bushes that were on the edge of the forest, near the

King's camp. He scanned the area and tried to find King Nikolai, who wielded the sword with the Gem that his master was so worried about. But he had a different goal in mind. He wouldn't kill the King. He would take advantage of this opportunity and let King Nikolai end his master's life, so that Draykon can finally steal the book of darkness that his master held so close to him nowadays. With that book, he would head back to his own country and create an army so powerful, he would take the Kingdom of Keya within a day.

Draykon smirked to himself. He knew what he needed to do.

Draykon lowered himself into the bushes as he heard movement up ahead, and was baffled when he saw the King. He looked so young, and yet he held so much power that could easily end his master's reign. Looking around the camp he spotted multiple guards standing near the King, but very few at the medical tent. Draykon let out a toothy snarl, getting his toxin ready for his first victim. He crawled forward, slowly, and carefully to the medical tent without making a sound. Once he was close enough to the nearest guard, he extended his mouth and bit down hard into one of the guard's legs. The guard yelped and looked down to see the culprit snarling back up at him. The guard moved back dizzily and tumbled to the ground, groaning as the toxin spread though his body slowly. The guard was paralysed by fear and the toxin, as the massive lizard dragged his body back into the bushes.

"One down," Draykon sneered.

Draykon then made his way over to the second guard, but stopped and watched as a person walked out from the tent followed by another figure. He watched as the older man looked around to see if anyone had seen him leave, then took out a flask from his pocket and drank the contents inside.

"Dad," Finnick said, walking up to his father.

"Son," Lord Hain, said wiping his mouth.

"Please don't tell me that's alcohol your drinking," Finnick said angrily.

"Son," Lord Hain began.

"Dad, we are in the middle of a war," Finnick said angrily. "You can't be drinking at a time like this."

"Do not tell me what I can and cannot do boy. I am your father," Lord Hain yelled.

"You've never been much of a father to me," Finnick stated. "You're always off drinking somewhere with your lady friends. Did you even care for mother? Or did you just use her for one night, then ignore her when you found out she was pregnant."

Finnick stared at his father as he waited for a reply. When none came, he walked away angrily. "Forget it."

Lord Hain watched his son walk away, then took out his flask and drank from it again, coughing as he drank the alcohol too quickly. Draykon crawled up quietly behind Lord Hain, then bit his leg and dragged him to the ground forcefully.

"Argh-, what the?" Lord Hain said, with a slur in his voice.

Lord Hain looked up while massaging the lump on his head, and saw a massive grey lizard staring right back at him, while pinning his legs to the ground. Lord Hain, fearing for his life, started to move back but couldn't as the massive lizard let go of his foot and climbed up onto Lord Hain's body and bit down onto his shoulder, hard.

Lord Hain screamed in pain.

The lizard moved to his arm and bit down once again, making sure this human had enough of his venom inside of him that he would suffer and eventually die.

"HEY, YOU!!!"

Draykon looked up and winced at the lights being lit up all around him and within the campsite. They had found him. Among the people who had gathered around him with their weapons pointed at him, were the Princess from Kudzu who could communicate with animals. He had been found.

"What is it?" Finnick asked.

"It's a Komodo Dragon. The largest known lizard in the world. Its bite is venomous, and its body is made of armoured scales. It's also known to be very strong," Iris whispered between them.

"Very wise, pretty girl," Draykon sneered.

"What do you want?" Nikolai yelled to the lizard.

"The one who holds the Crystal Gem," Draykon said.

"Why?" Issac called out.

"My Master wishes for me to kill the one who owns it," Draykon said evenly.

"At least he's honest," Finnick said.

"So, which one is it?" Draykon said, knowing full well who it was.

Draykon wanted to buy as much time as he could, so the venom would be too late to heal for the human behind him.

"Your fight is with-," Nikolai began, but was interrupted by another voice.

"With me lizard," King Jabari said withdrawing his sword. "Get Lord Hain to the medical tent. If the Princess is right about the venom, Lord Hain's life is in danger."

The others nodded their understanding, but Nikolai stood his ground staring at King Jabari with concern.

"You are still young, King Nikolai. Let me fight this battle for you," King Jabari pleaded. "It would be my honour."

Nikolai nodded and moved back with the others, waiting for the right time to get to Lord Hain without getting bitten by the lizard.

"How interesting," Draykon observed.

Draykon smiled at King Jabari then stood up on his hind legs. He positioned his tail right behind him so he could stand upright without falling. King Jabari stood back shocked at how tall that now made Draykon.

Draykon laughed with glee.

"Bet you didn't know I could do that," Draykon scorned.

King Jabari composed himself then stood ready to attack, sword in both hands.

Draykon ran up to King Jabari with his claws out and ready to bite. Once he got close enough to strike, he attempted to claw at King Jabari, but the King held his sword in a defence position, protecting his torso from harm. Draykon hissed at King Jabari, showing his long yellow forked tongue. King Jabari, disgusted at the sight, used his kingdom's Gem strength to push the lizard away by force. Omari then came in and punched the lizard hard enough that it landed in a tree metres away.

"Nice job son," King Jabari praised.

"Thanks dad," Omari said bumping his fists together.

"Take Lord Hain to the medical tent. We will finish this battle," King Jabari urged.

Finnick, Nikolai and Issac rushed over to the unconscious Lord Hain. Picking him up they quickly hurried him over to the medical tent. Once they entered the tent, Juliet and Julia came running up to them with a look of concern between them.

"Over on that bed," Queen Julia ordered the men.

The men swiftly and cautiously moved the unconscious Lord Hain to the bed, then stepped back to let the healers perform their work. The two queens promptly donned aprons and rolled up their sleeves before examining the victims' wounds in detail.

"Juliet, you attend to his left shoulder, I'll start on his right," Queen Julia instructed.

"Okay," Juliet said, placing her hand over Lord Hain's wound.

After healing Lord Hain for a few minutes, worry tore at Queen Julia. There was too much poison, making it unlikely they could save him. Thinking the same, Juliet spoke up about another option.

"One potential option is cilantro, which contains a chemical compound that binds to toxic metals and aids the body in their elimination. It could help him and give us time to save him," Juliet explained to her mother.

"Good idea. Let's give it a go." Queen Julia said, then called to one of the female volunteers.

They rushed to stand before the Queen and bowed. "How can I help, Your Highness?"

"I need you to get some cilantro from the herb table. Crush it and add it to water for Lord Hain. It will help his body fight off the poison," Queen Julia instructed.

"Of course," the volunteer replied, rushing off to gather the herb.

Julia sighed, fearing the worst, but continued to do her duty to save Lord Hain.

A couple of metres away Issac watched as Julia healed the deep wounds on Lord Hain's body. Concern etched his forehead. When he helped bring Lord Hain inside the medical tent he could smell alcohol on his breath.

Why was he drinking at a crucial time like this? Especially since we're in a middle of a war, he thought.

He turned to one of the volunteers who was standing around and waiting for orders. They looked his way, and he beckoned them to come over.

"Tell Lieutenant Riely I need to see her," Issac ordered.

Lieutenant Riley came in minutes later and stood in front of her Captain.

"I need you, Finnick and Jarreth to scout the surrounding area. We just had a breach," Issac ordered. "Be careful, King Jabari and Prince Omari are fighting with the intruder."

"Yes sir," Riley said, rushing off to complete the task.

Finnick looked at his father with concern one more time before following Riley.

"I'll stand guard outside with Captain Chase, while you watch in here," Issac said to Nikolai.

"Good plan," Nikolai said nodding.

Lord Hain started coughing and white foam frothed from his mouth. His body started to spasm from the venom spreading inside.

"Quick, roll him on his side otherwise he'll choke," Queen Julia ordered Nikolai.

Nikolai rolled Lord Hain onto his side to help clear his airways so he could breathe properly. Queen Julia then bent over and inspected Lord Hain's condition. She checked his eyes, pulse, and breathing then she stood back with a grim look and shook her head.

"Roll him back," Queen Julia said.

Nikolai, with the help of Juliet, laid Lord Hain's body back onto the bed. Queen Julia reached over and closed his eyes and put a sheet over his body, head to toe.

"He's dead," Queen Julia whispered.

"Dead?" Nikolai asked.

"What," Juliet sighed, leaning on the bench exhausted.

"There was enough poison inside him to kill three humans. The herb wouldn't have made a difference," Queen Julia explained.

"You did what you could," Nikolai said, then walked up to Juliet as she leaned on him for support. "Both of you."

Oberon came in and saw the scene before him after hearing from another soldier what had happened. Seeing the healers standing back with Lord Hain covered in a white sheet, Oberon knew it was too late.

"I'll go and tell the lad," Oberon said.

Oberon sighed to himself as he exited the tent. He saw Finnick running around the perimeter with his axe in hand, checking for any more breaches. He hesitated for a moment before he ran over to Finnick. As he ran, he tried to think of an uncomplicated way for him to break the news to his lieutenant.

CHAPTER TWENTY-SEVEN

"The righteous perish, and no one takes it to heart;
the religious are taken away, and no one understands
that the righteous are taken away to be spared from evil."

Isaiah 57

King Jabari placed his hand over his wounded arm and winced. The Komodo Dragon had managed to get him during the last encounter. Watching his son fight with the lizard, he quickly pulled his jacket sleeve over his wound to hide it from him. He needed to finish this battle soon before the poison took effect on his body, then he could get treated. He wasn't going to abandon his son on the battlefield, especially to this lizard.

He looked down at his wound again. "Just a small scratch, I have plenty of time."

Switching his sword to his uninjured hand he ran up to his son, just as he landed another punch towards the lizard's chest, making it stumble back against the tree.

"You're a strong one, aren't you? Not many people can stay in a fight with me," Draykon admired. "But you're not normal. I was told that your kingdom's Gem has the power of strength."

"That's right, and I'll beat you with the power the God of Light has generously given us," Omari said angrily.

"Ohh I'm terrified," Draykon mocked.

"Easy son, he's trying to taunt you into fighting recklessly," King Jabari warned, standing next to his son.

Draykon smirked at King Jabari and looked to his arm.

"Don't worry, this battle will end soon enough," Draykon said lunging forward again.

Prince Omari and King Jabari split apart a second before Draykon clawed at them. Turning around King Jabari brought down his sword onto Draykon's dragon like body, but nothing happened. Draykon snickered.

"Damn it," King Jabari said moving back quickly. "Get back son."

"What's wrong father?" Omari said, distancing himself.

"Remember what Princess Iris said. Its body is made of armoured scales. My sword, with my strength, couldn't even penetrate it," King Jabari said, puffing as he clutched his arm.

"Father, are you okay?" Omari asked, seeing him in distress.

"Not long now," Draykon laughed.

"What did you do?" Omari yelled, starting to walk towards Draykon.

"Son," King Jabari yelled. "Calm down, he's taunting you."

Omari stopped and turned to his father, only to see him panting and sweating. He knew something was wrong. Running over, he looked at his father with concern.

"It's just a scratch," King Jabari told his son.

"No," Omari said worriedly. "You need to get to the medical tent and get treated fast."

"And leave you here with him," King Jabari nodded to Draykon. "No, I will finish this fight."

"Excellent," Draykon sneered.

Draykon didn't wait as he ran towards them again with his claws out and teeth bared. King Jabari saw that the lizard was focused on his son, and at the last minute pushed Omari out of the way, and away from Draykon's reach. Draykon bit down hard into King Jabari's shoulder and left his teeth in his flesh a bit longer than usual, to let the venom spread quicker.

"FATHER!!!!!!!," Omari yelled.

Draykon let go and backed away just as King Jabari fell to the ground, blood pouring out of his wound, and froth coming out of his mouth. Omari ran over to his father while calling out for help. Nikolai and Finnick ran out of the tent after hearing him call out, seeing Omari run towards his father.

"King Jabari," Nikolai yelled as he ran over.

"Omari," Finnick called, following behind Nikolai.

"My father," Omari began.

Suddenly, a high pitch noise sounded across the battlefield. All eyes darted around to find the source of the sound. Nikolai looked towards Draykon as the lizard stood up and looked over to the hill where his master sat. Nikolai looked in the same direction as Draykon, but couldn't see any movement in the darkness. Looking back at the lizard, Draykon sneered at Nikolai before getting on all fours again and retreating to his master.

"Next time."

Nikolai looked back to Omari who was kneeling by his father's side.

"Quick take him to Juliet," Nikolai ordered.

Finnick, Nikolai and Omari helped King Jabari to his feet, and they all stumbled to the medical tent.

"Juliet," Nikolai called as they went inside.

"What happened?" Queen Julia asked.

"The lizard got to him," Omari sniffed.

"Juliet," Queen Julia called.

"Coming," Juliet said, pulling her hair back.

"Put him on the table," Queen Julia ordered.

As Finnick, Nikolai and Omari took King Jabari to the nearest bed, Queen Nala stirred from the next bed over. Slowly opening her eyes, she saw her husband lying on the bed beside her, foaming and thrashing due to the venom inside of him.

"My love," Queen Nala whispered.

"Mum," Omari said, rushing to her side.

"Is he okay?" she asked.

"I don't know," Omari sniffed.

"Alright everybody please clear the area," Queen Julia said, coming over to King Jabari's bed.

Juliet followed over with the mortar and pestle in her hand. The cilantro that was meant for Lord Hain was still unused and could be used for King Jabari in his condition. Juliet stood by King Jabari's beside.

"God of Light. I pray this works," Juliet prayed.

After the froth was cleared, Juliet nodded to Nikolai, who supported King Jabari's head as Juliet put the mortar to the King's mouth.

"Open up Your Highness," Juliet encouraged.

King Jabari opened his mouth and began drinking the herb. After he had finished, Juliet nodded to Nikolai and he laid King Jabari's head back down. Queen Julia and Juliet began rushing to heal King Jabari's wound, praying that the herb and their healing abilities combined would help the King.

As both mother and daughter healed the King, Omari and Queen Nala watched from the next bed over. Both held onto the hope that they would see the King live. After a few minutes of healing, Omari couldn't wait and asked Juliet about his father's condition.

"I think he'll be okay," Juliet said, checking with her mother.

"I agree. He didn't have nowhere near as much poison as Lord Hain had in him," Queen Julia agreed.

Relief showed on both Omari's and his mother's face as they both wiped the tears from their eyes, grateful to both Queens.

King Jabari then coughed and started breathing normally again. He opened his eyes and looked around the room.

"What happened?" King Jabari asked.

"Dad," Omari laughed, while hugging his father.

"Son," King Jabari said, hugging his son.

"Juliet and I managed to heal you just in time before the poison took over," Queen Julia said, smiling at her daughter.

"We were worried because of the poison. Lord Hain had a lot in him whereas you didn't, you were easily treated whereas Lord Hain wasn't," Juliet turned to Finnick. "I'm sorry about your father."

"It's not your fault," Finnick reassured. "He was careless."

"Careless," Queen Julia said concerned. "Finnick, he was still your father."

"He was drunk. I caught him drinking before he got attacked. If he wasn't careless, he would still be alive," Finnick stated, then cleared his throat. "Your Highness."

"It's true," Issac agreed. "I smelt it on his breath when we carried him inside."

"Oh my," Queen Julia gasped. "I'm sorry lieutenant."

"It's okay," Finnick said softly.

King Jabari sat up in bed and took a deep breath in, then exhaled.

"Wow, I feel great. Amazing gift your kingdom has. Thank you," King Jabari laughed.

"We owe it all to the God of Light," Juliet said smiling.

Queen Julia smiled as she watched her daughter walk off, then she turned back to the others.

"Any news on what that high pitch sound was?" Queen Julia asked.

"I'll go and check," Finnick said.

Finnick walked out of the tent then came back minutes later with Jarreth and Iris in tow.

"Any news?" Issac asked.

"Nothing so far. Captain Oberon and his men are on watch and would like Issac and his men to take over in a few hours," Jarreth signed to everyone.

"My animal friends who are nocturnal are keeping watch as well, the first sign of movement and we will know," Iris said with confidence.

"Alright everyone, get some rest. We don't know when the second wave will come," Nikolai told the group.

✦ ✦ ✦ ✦ ✦

A horn blew loudly throughout the campsite, waking everybody up. Soldiers picked up their weapons and lined up behind there captains, waiting for an order. Juliet ran to the medical tent to where her mother stood at the front, waiting to hear what was happening. Nikolai, with his sword in hand, ran up to Oberon, Kirsten, and Issac to hear the news.

"What's happening?" Nikolai asked.

"Movement in the enemy camp," Kirsten said. "My soldiers saw the Prince of Darkness assembling his followers."

"And the creatures?" Issac asked.

"Standing behind him and ready," Kirsten said, worried.

"What creatures has he summoned this time?" Nikolai was afraid to ask.

Oberon sighed as he rubbed his forehead.

"You remember those spiders we fought that belonged to Jorogumo, her guard spiders?" Oberon asked.

"The massive ones," Nikolai said.

"Think bigger than that," Oberon said.

"Damn," Nikolai shuddered.

"He's also summoned a cerberus and many werebats," Oberon shared.

"A werebat?" Nikolai asked confused.

Kirsten, Issac, and Oberon shared a look of disgust and worry.

"Werebats are a grotesque creature. Once human, but after the Prince of Darkness has experimented on them, they no longer are. They look like a giant bat, and are a little taller and bulkier looking than a human. They are said to have great hearing, sharp claws and teeth, and can obviously fly," Kirsten explained.

"Nasty creatures, all of them," Issac said.

"So that's all the creatures the Prince of Darkness has summoned?" Nikolai asked.

"Yes," Kirsten replied.

"Only three?" Nikolai asked.

"There are three species, but he has summoned an army of them, plus his followers," Kirsten said.

"What are your orders, Your Highness?" Oberon said standing beside him.

"When fighting the creatures, we need to do it in a team. These creatures are deadlier and bigger than the first wave. No one goes at it alone. Understood," Nikolai ordered.

"Yes sir," Oberon, Kirsten and Issac said, before leaving to inform their soldiers.

✦ ✦ ✦ ✦ ✦

One the other side of the battlefield, the Prince of Darkness glared down at the lowly humans who had rejected him and his power. Watching them frantically prepare for their next attack, he smiled at their fear. Their hopes will be crushed soon enough, and they will finally learn to give up altogether when he wins this war. And when he wins, he will make them suffer as punishment for defying him in the first place.

"Master, I almost had him," Draykon said, coming up and bowing.

"No, it was pointless. There was no way you would be fighting Nikolai. They know he's the key into defeating me. That's why the King of Neylon fought you instead," the Prince of Darkness said.

"If you would have given me more time, I would have made it to Nikolai," Draykon said sternly.

The Prince of Darkness turned and looked to Draykon and glared at him. He wanted to kill him for questioning his decisions, but thought he better not as he still needed Draykon as a pawn in his games.

"Of course, you know better Master," Draykon said backing down.

"I do," was all the Prince of Darkness said.

Draykon sneered and turned from his master.

Not now, later, he thought.

He went over to the other followers who stood behind their master and waited with them for his next order. The Prince of Darkness continued to watch the campsite, and all the humans who would soon bow down to him. He looked over to Nikolai who was staring at him. The Prince of Darkness smirked and held his head high.

He smiled to himself. "It is time."

The Prince of Darkness turned and faced his followers and looked at each of them. His followers and creatures were all unsettled at all the waiting, but the time to strike was now. They didn't need to wait anymore.

"Rise my beasts, and destroy the pure hearted," he ordered "But leave King Nikolai to me."

His followers and creatures yelled and roared as they began descending the hill and into the battlefield, leaving their master behind as he slowly walked down. The Prince of Darkness watched the battle unfold below, and anyone who came to close to him saw his blade for the last time. Follower or not.

Back at the medical tent, Nikolai watched the Prince of Darkness walk down towards the battlefield, then stop and look directly at him. He smirked at him, then held his sword of darkness in an attack position for a second, before running straight for Nikolai.

"Let's finish this," Nikolai whispered.

Nikolai took out his own sword and activated the Crystal gem, then began walking towards the Prince of Darkness. Coming up from his right-side, Nikolai saw a giant spider coming straight for him from the battlefield. Slicing the beast in an x formation, he walked past it's dead body without any remorse. His eyes focused on the Prince of Darkness, as he held his sword firmly in his hands.

CHAPTER TWENTY-EIGHT

"Finally, be strong in the Lord and in his mighty power."

Ephesians 6

Jarreth shot his arrows with speed, trying his hardest to keep up with the incoming attacks from the creatures and evil followers. He ended up back-to-back with Finnick and Iris, each defending one another from attacks, from each other's blind spots.

"Hey Jarreth," Finnick called, swinging his axe, slicing another spider.

Jarreth turned to face Finnick, shooting an arrow towards his friend, which whizzed past him, hitting a werebat coming from behind.

"*What*," Jarreth signed.

"Behind you," Finnick shouted, slicing at the spider they were fighting together.

Jarreth turned and shot an arrow at another incoming giant spider.

"Man, they don't seem to stop," Finnick said, getting flustered. Jarreth stopped fighting and turned towards his friend.

"*Just think about the holiday we'll take after,*" Jarreth signed, smiling at his friend.

"Roast and beer. Roast and beer," Finnick kept telling himself, then swung his axe at another incoming spider.

Jarreth smiled at Finnick while he took another arrow out. He shot at the incoming werebats chest, as Finnick sliced off its wing. They celebrated their small victory with a high five, as another werebat fell dead to the ground. Iris turned to her friends to say something, but stopped when she saw what was coming up from behind both lieutenants. She ran up to them with her daggers raised.

"Mala," she called to one of her tiger friends.

Mala, a female tiger ran up to Princess Iris coming in close beside her. Iris laid her hand onto Mala's forehead, and used her amethyst Gem to take on the abilities of a tiger. Her hands transformed into claws, her speed became faster, her sharp teeth showed when she smiled, and tiger ears popped up onto her head as she listened for danger.

"Guys," Iris shouted again.

Both lieutenants turned to find Iris running up and pointing behind them. They turned to see what was coming up from behind them. They both readied their weapons as Draykon, in his Komodo Dragon form, ran up to them with his teeth barred. Jarreth began shooting his arrows one by one, trying to hit Draykon. But his armoured skin was too thick, and his arrows kept bouncing off, having no effect. Finnick used his huge axe as a shield as Draykon's claw came down towards his leg. Holding Draykon back with his giant axe, Finnick struggled to keep him away from him, knowing full well what this creature did to his father.

"My, my, you look familiar," Draykon said smiling, his eye's lighting up at the sudden realisation. "Young Lord Hain."

Using his giant axe, Finnick pushed Draykon away forcefully, then moved back to rejoin Jarreth and Iris. They all stood side by side as Draykon stared at them hungrily.

"Be careful guys, Komodo Dragons are dangerous," Iris whispered, with her claws ready.

Jarreth got another arrow out and readied his bow at Draykon.

"Is his whole body armoured?" Finnick whispered to Iris.

"His weak spots are his eyes, mouth and nose," Iris whispered back.

"Right, I have a plan, but it will be risky," Finnick announced to his friends.

From a few metres away Draykon watched with curiosity as Finnick, Jarreth and Iris whispered amongst themselves while still watching him. Draykon smiled at himself at how smart the young Lord Hain was compared to his father. He stood there trying to read their lips and figure out their plan, but it was harder than it looked. The three broke their conversation and moved away from one another and surrounded Draykon. Finnick went to Draykon's left side while Iris went to his right side. Draykon looked ahead and saw Jarreth running away from him and the others, and thought it was odd.

He is ditching his friends. I guess war changes people, Draykon thought.

Draykon started running after Jarreth, and in no time at all, closed the distance between them quickly. He was about to take a bite, when Finnick came up from behind and brought his axe down towards Draykon's body. Draykon moved aside quickly and spun around, using his tail to trip Finnick. Draykon backed away and tried to find the princess. He turned around frantically and found Iris coming at him head on. Her sharp claws sliced the side of his mouth, then she backed away quickly, as Draykon tried to use his own claws on her. Draykon touched the fresh wound and saw that he was bleeding. Licking his lips he could taste blood.

He smiled. "You're stronger than you look."

"I'll take that as a compliment," Iris said, posing for another attack.

Draykon smiled, showing his long yellow forked tongue and sharp teeth.

"Hey," Finnick called, getting Draykon's attention.

Draykon turned and lunged at Finnick who quickly moved out of the way, and used his axe on Draykon's armoured body. Draykon turned quickly and tripped Finnick over again with his tail.

"Will you ever learn?" Draykon hissed. "I thought you were the smart young Lord."

"Ouch," Finnick said, landing on the ground hard.

Draykon saw the opportunity that Finnick was defenceless and without his weapon. So, he ran over to him and placed his long claw onto Finnick's chest, preventing him from moving. Draykon bent over his prey with his teeth exposed, saliva running down his mouth and ready to attack.

"Big mistake, young Lord Hain," Draykon snickered, putting pressure onto Finnick's chest.

"That's my line," Finnick groaned.

"What," Draykon said confused.

Finnick smiled and pointed upwards. Draykon grumbled then looked up, keeping the pressure on Finnick. His eyes went wide with fear, and he quickly removed his claws.

Woosh.

"Aghhhhh," Draykon yelled, moving away from Finnick.

Jarreth, re-sheathing his bow and arrow ran over and helped Finnick up. Both lieutenants looked over to Draykon, who was screaming in pain at the arrow sticking out from his eye. Iris came up and stood in defence beside the two men.

"Nice shooting," she praised Jarreth.

"*Thanks*," Jarreth signed.

Draykon yelled in pain and moved away from Jarreth, Iris and Finnick. Once he was a safe distance away, he tried to pull out the arrow, but stopped as it caused him even more pain. Cautious about doing more damage to his eye, he left the arrow inside and glared furiously at Jarreth.

The battle was not over.

"Not so high and mighty now," Finnick yelled. "Looks like every person has their weakness, and we just found yours."

Draykon glared at Jarreth with fury, but deep inside he feared for his life. These worthless humans knew his weakness. He needed to leave. Live today and fight another day. He only faked his allegiance to the Dark One to gain more power, so there was no way he was going to die for him.

"This is not over," Draykon said, fleeing from the battlefield.

Iris, Jarreth and Finnick watched Draykon flee, then smiled amongst themselves over their small victory.

"Nice plan Finnick," Iris praised, giving him a high five. "Nice shooting Jarreth." Iris smiled then kissed Jarreth quickly on the cheek.

"*Thank you*," Jarreth mouthed to Iris as he gave her a side hug.

Jarreth turned to Finnick and signed. "*Are you okay? Are you hurt?*"

"Nah, I'm good," Finnick said, smiling smugly at his friend with the princess.

"*What*," Jarreth said, signing to his friend.

"Nothing," Finnick said, then began to laugh.

Oberon swung his broadsword at the incoming werebat, and with help from Issac they managed to defeat another creature of darkness. Oberon removed his sword from the werebats chest and watched the beast fall to the ground. Turning around he walked over to Issac and gave him a hand up.

"You okay, Your Highness?" Oberon asked.

"Yes, thank you Captain," Issac said, wiping the blood from his cheek.

Oberon stood beside Issac and watched the battlefield that surrounded them. People from each kingdom had come together to fight alongside the animals and the alicorn race, to defeat the evil that had invaded their peace. Each were fighting side by side as the battle raged on, taking heavy losses on both sides. Issac nudged Oberon and pointed to their right. Oberon looked over to see two more werebats flying towards them.

"Ready for round two," Issac said taking out his sword.

"More like round ten," Oberon said, giving a small laugh, as he stretched his muscles.

Issac laughed. "Yeah, it does feel like that."

The werebats flew up to both Oberon and Issac screeching, with their sharp claws swiping at both Captains. Oberon wincing at his own wounds, quickly turned, and sliced at one of the werebats. The werebat screeched from its own wound then crashed onto the ground whimpering, then went silent once Oberon rushed over to finished the job. Issac sliced the wings off the werebat he was fighting, so it wouldn't escape. With injured wings, the creature used its claws and strength to slice multiple times at Issac, who winced from the impact, unable to avoid all the attacks. Oberon came up from behind the creature and thrusted his sword into the werebats stomach.

"Thanks," Issac said. "You're hurt. You should get that looked at."

Oberon saw the multiple wounds on his arms and shrugged. "Just cuts. I'll be fine, what about you?" Oberon asked, looking over at Issac's wounds.

"I'll be fine," Issac said, bandaging up his arm. "Do you want to bandage up your arms, to stop the bleeding?" Issac offered, giving him some of his own bandages.

"You carry that stuff around?" Oberon asked, amused.

Issac smiled. "My wife is a healer. She never lets me leave home without it."

Oberon and Issac shared a brief moment of peace as they both shared a laugh, while each bandaging their own wounds to prevent anymore bleeding. Issac then wiped the sweat from his forehead and puffed, exhaustion finally hitting him. From the corner of his eye, he saw movement. Turning, he saw two massive spiders scuttling towards the medical tent.

"Julia, Juliet," Issac said in fear.

"Go," Oberon said, throwing the bandage back to Issac. "I'll hold the others off from here."

"Thanks Captain," Issac said, running towards the medical tent.

Captain Oberon turned around and groaned silently. The three headed Cerberus was headed straight for him. From a distance he saw King Jabari, Prince Omari and Captain Chase noticing the massive beast running closer towards him. All ran in his direction each with their own weapons raised. Relief washed over him as he was glad he wasn't fighting this fearsome beast alone.

Issac ran towards the tent, with his newfound energy. His wife and stepdaughter were inside, and he would protect them at all costs. Upon entering the tent entrance, he quickly stood back as he saw something big fly past him. Turning around he saw the giant spider covered in vines, strapped against a tree, struggling to escape. He looked inside to find Juliet using her earth Gem's abilities to trap the second giant spider from attacking a volunteer. Cowering against the tent wall, the volunteer looked terrified as

Juliet held off one giant spider inside, and the other outside. An idea struck Juliet as she saw her Venus Fly Trap opening its plant mouth again, hungry for more. Juliet left the vines intact that were constricting the giant spider as it's victim. She turned and walked over to her plant. Placing both hands onto the plant, she focused on her earth abilities. The Venus Fly Trap began to grow, as its long leaf blades became bigger as the plant grew taller. Juliet removed her hands and took a step back at her now massive plant and smiled. The plant was big enough for these two new massive additions. Turning around she saw Issac and smiled.

"Do you like the new security measures for the medical tent?" Juliet asked laughing.

"I was worried for no reason," Issac said, looking at the massive plant.

Juliet turned to the volunteer and saw her mother kneeling next to the women, and giving her some water.

"Are you okay?"

"Yes. Thank you, Your Highness," the volunteer said, eyeing the restrained spider.

"Are those the same ones from the Kingdom of Kudzu?" Julia asked.

"No, these are bigger," Juliet said, shivering at the thought. "Alright. Now to get rid of these two."

She started with the spider inside the tent, and dropped it into the plant's open leaf blade mouth. The plants mouth shut as soon as the spider was dropped inside, and Juliet and Issac watched as the plant tightened its grip and ate the spider.

"How long will it take to digest?" Issac asked, amazed.

"Considering how big the spider is, maybe a while," Juliet guessed.

"And the spider outside is safe for the time being?" Issac asked, looking behind him.

"Yes. Those vines aren't loosening anytime soon," Juliet encouraged, then faltered, grabbing the nearest table.

Queen Julia jumped up and ran to her daughter, while the volunteer got a chair and brought it over.

"Are you okay?" Issac asked, lowering Juliet into the chair.

"Just feeling a bit dizzy," Juliet replied.

"You've been at this all day. Rest Juliet," her mother encouraged.

Feeling drained by the extra use of her Gem, Juliet listened to her mother and rested in the chair provided. Issac, feeling concerned for his family's safety turned and left the tent. After the volunteer gave some water to Juliet she left to do some work. Queen Julia held her daughter's hand with concern, knowing the toll it took on someone's body when they used to much of the Gem's abilities. Before Queen Julia could say anything, she and Juliet looked towards the tent entrance with curiosity as they heard a loud thud outside. Minutes later Issac came in re-sheathing his sword and walked over to them both.

"The spider?" Queen Julia asked.

"Dead. Sorry, I couldn't take any chances with both of you so exhausted already," Issac apologised.

"Thank you, Issac," Juliet whispered, exhausted.

"Thank you," Queen Julia said tearily.

"Anytime. How are you both?" Issac asked his wife, then he looked at Juliet seeing how tired she was.

"Exhausted, after fighting and healing people. I just hope this war ends soon," Queen Julia said, cuddling her daughter, while holding her husband's hand.

"I'm okay mother. I just used too much energy. After a good rest I'll be able to help again," Juliet said, then yawned as her eyes slowly drooped to a close.

"Rest, Juliet," Queen Julia said, watching her daughter sleep.

Queen Julia turned to Issac and smiled at him while caressing his face.

Then out of nowhere a huge gush of wind passed without warning. The medical tent bent with such force from the wind, it almost broke. Empty beds and tables were knocked over, while the occupied moved a couple of centimetres. The King and Queen looked around at the frightened volunteers and wounded. No one was hurt and thankfully Juliet had slept through the ordeal.

"What's going on?" Queen Julia said panicked, hugging Juliet.

Issac jumped up and ran out of the tent. Stopping outside he saw enemies and allies knocked to the ground mid battle. Lieutenant Riely stumbled up and helped Captain Chase up, before they both ran towards to Captain Issac.

"What happened?" Issac asked, meeting them halfway.

"I don't know," Lieutenant Riely reported.

"Up there," shouted Omari from the battlefield.

Looking up towards the mountain where the Prince of Darkness once stood, he saw King Nikolai and the Dark One kneeling on opposites sides, breathless from the exhaustion their swords had caused during the recent impact. The Dark One's sword was surrounded with a black mist, while Nikolai's sword was surrounded in white flames as the Crystal Gem shone brightly. The impact from the two powerful swords, made the ground shake and the wind blow with force.

It was enough to cause casualties, even death, if anyone was unlucky to be close enough to the impact.

CHAPTER TWENTY-NINE

"For God is not a God of disorder but of peace."

1 Corinthians 14:33

With his sword firmly embedded into the ground, Nikolai held onto the sword's hilt until the strong impact was gone. Looking up he saw the Prince of Darkness on the opposite side kneeling, and clutching at his sword as well.

"Well, well, well," the Prince of Darkness smirked. "That was something." The Prince of Darkness looked around at the damage the two swords had done upon impact and smiled to himself. "Nice sword you got there."

Nikolai stood up while staring at the Prince of Darkness. He pulled his sword out from the ground and raised it up towards the Dark One.

"What, no words for a god," the Prince of Darkness laughed. "I would be speechless too if I were in the presence of the divine god."

"You are no god," Nikolai said sternly, clutching his sword.

The Prince of Darkness looked at Nikolai and laughed, then

his expression softened as he held his hand to his heart.

"My boy, you've been deceived," the Prince of Darkness began.

"No, I haven't. You have killed thousands of people throughout the years, experimenting on many of them in horrible ways. You cause fear and panic amongst us, and lie for your own benefit," Nikolai stated. "You are no god. The God of Light banished you to the cave of Akuma. To live shackled, and weak, in the darkness you so crave for eternity, for the evil you have brought upon us and your betrayal to him."

"Yes well, I managed to escape and now that I'm back I want my revenge," the Prince of Darkness said raising his sword. "And I will have my way."

Nikolai stood in a long stance position with his sword ready to attack and defend. It took him no time to activate the Crystal Gem within his sword, making his sword dance with white flames. The Prince of Darkness ran up to Nikolai and thrust his sword towards him. Quickly dodging the attack Nikolai moved sideways and brought his sword down towards the Prince of Darkness's arm. Missing by mere inches the Prince of Darkness laughed as he backed away, swinging his sword casually as he admired the young King.

"You're a worthy opponent," the Prince of Darkness acknowledged.

Nikolai ignored him and stood ready, knowing full well the Prince of Darkness was trying to distract him.

"I could use your strength on my team," the Prince of Darkness offered.

"Not a chance," Nikolai said.

"Why?" the Prince of Darkness asked. "I'll give you everything and anything you've ever wanted."

"No thanks, I have everything I need," Nikolai said. "And I

choose to serve the God of Light."

"You'll regret that," the Prince of Darkness growled.

"No, I won't," Nikolai said, running forward with his sword raised.

Nikolai slashed at the Dark One continuously, missing every time he tried to land a direct hit. The Dark One blocked or dodged his every move with a smile on his face, and Nikolai began to feel hopeless as the battle wore on. He felt that he was just a normal person, whereas the Prince of Darkness used to be the right-hand person to the God of Light, before his betrayal. This made him strong and powerful, and Nikolai felt he was no match for him. Moving back, Nikolai kept his distance, panting and sweating with exhaustion while the Prince of Darkness looked at him smiling and unaffected.

"You know this could end differently," the Prince of Darkness said smiling. "We could end this right now."

Nikolai shook his head, knowing full well that the Dark One was trying to make him change sides. "No."

"Look around you, look at how much death and destruction there is. All that could end with one simple word," the Prince of Darkness explained. "Will you join me?"

Nikolai looked at the Prince of Darkness's offered hand, then looked at the battlefield around him. Allies fought with bravery, courage, and determination, hoping to win this war. Humans, animals and alicorn's fought side by side together. But after fighting with the Prince of Darkness, Nikolai started to lose faith in winning. He thought about his wife Juliet, and of their future. He thought about his friend, Theo, who had supported him throughout his years growing up with his curse. He thought about his parents and all they had given up for him. He also thought about all the new friends and family he had gained while on this quest for peace.

"Trust in the God of Light," Nikolai heard Malachi's words echo through his mind.

Nikolai sighed. He knew only one way to end this war. He didn't like it, but it was his only option at this time. He looked over the battlefield to his friends and allies, then to the medical tent where his wife was. He then saw the last fearsome beast that the soldiers had trouble killing. The Cerberus. He saw King Jabari with his son Prince Omari trying to hold the three headed beast back, as Captain Oberon and Captain Chase planted multiple strikes against the beast, which resulted in little damage. The only way the beast would disappear would be when the Dark One was defeated. Nikolai took in a long breath, then let it out. He knew what he had to do.

"I love you Juliet," Nikolai whispered to himself.

Nikolai looked back over to the Prince of Darkness's offered hand and sighed.

"Will you join me Nikolai?" the Prince of Darkness asked again.

"Over my dead body," Nikolai plainly said.

The Prince of Darkness's face turned to anger. "That can be arranged."

The Dark One ran up to Nikolai and attacked, sneering at him, his victory at hand. Sharp pains erupted from Nikolai, and he let out a yell that carried across the battlefield. His stomach became warm and wet, and he suddenly felt very dizzy. When Nikolai felt his stomach, his hand became covered with blood. He smiled as blood dripped from his mouth, as he staggered forward.

His plan had worked.

After battling with the Dark One and not getting close enough to injure him, Nikolai had finally done it. His plan had finally worked. Looking up he smiled at the Prince of Darkness.

"What's so fun-," the Prince of Darkness began.

The Dark One grunted in pain as he felt and saw Nikolai's sword thrusted into his heart. Nikolai tried with all his strength to push the blade in as far as he could, but with his strength weakening he had only done so much. The Dark One had one hand on Nikolai's sword ready to pull it out.

"That won't kill m-," the Prince of Darkness began.

Nikolai quickly activated the Crystal Gem, engulfing his sword in white flames. The white flames surrounded the Prince of Darkness, triggering him to stumble back and scream as he became consumed by the flames. Nikolai stumbled to the ground while holding his stomach, as he watched the Prince of Darkness scream until he collapsed onto the ground unmoving. His body turned black, then turned to dust, and was swept away in the wind. Nikolai's body gave way as he collapsed to the ground, feeling his time was coming close to an end. He thought about Juliet, his friends and family, and how he would miss them. Choking back tears, Nikolai coughed again, the pain from his stomach sharpening. He winced as he tried to lessen the pain by pulling out the blade, but he had no strength left in him. He looked up towards the sky and started to close his eyes from tiredness, but was blinded by a bright light in a shape of a person coming towards him. The white being knelt in front of Nikolai and spoke softly.

"Nikolai," the soft voice said. "You are not alone."

"Malachi," Nikolai whispered.

Nikolai saw Malachi the angel smile at him before everything went dark.

✦ ✦ ✦ ✦ ✦

Draykon ran back up to the hill where his master stood once before. After fleeing the battle from the young Lord Hain and his friends, he had transformed back into his human self. He collapsed onto the ground and breathed heavily. His wounded eye was badly damaged, and the pain was unbearable. He would not stay here and die for the master; he needed to leave. He stood up and looked around; there was no one here at their base camp. He could easy leave without anyone knowing about it.

This is too easy, Draykon smiled to himself.

As he turned to the forest to flee, his good eye caught something black on the ground, among other belongings. As he walked over, he realised it was his masters Book of Darkness. The book where he had summoned his army of creatures for the war. Looking around again to make sure he was alone, Draykon took another step further and picked it up. He could feel the power that radiated from the book. This would be a great advantage for him. He could create his own army of creatures, this time being much stronger. Then he would march to the Kingdom of Keya and get revenge on his cousins. He looked at the front cover markings and thought they looked familiar, but couldn't remember where he had seen them previously. Before he could get a chance to look more into it, he heard sounds nearby. Fearing he would be discovered, he turned and bolted towards the forest that led out of the battlefield, and straight to the Kingdom of Zolatta. From there he could take passage in a ship and sail back to his home country.

He smiled to himself while clutching the book to his chest. "Finally."

After running for a while, the pain in his eye had gotten worse so Draykon stopped to rest. He stopped by a stream and sat with his back towards a tree and closed his eyes to rest. The pain in his eye throbbed now and Draykon was angry at Jarreth for the damage. Soon he will get his revenge on the mute, but first his he had to deal with the problem back home. There was rustling in the bushes as the wind picked up and Draykon was relieved the day was becoming cooler. A stick breaking nearby notified Draykon that someone was close. Standing up with the book close to his chest, Draykon looked around the forest that surrounded him.

"Come out whoever you are," Draykon ordered.

There was silence for a minute before two people came out from the bushes. They stood looking at the book which Draykon held so close to him.

"Where do you think you're going, traitor?" the female spat furiously.

"Can't you see that our Master is losing," Draykon informed. "King Nikolai has the Crystal Gem, our Master's weakness, open your eyes."

The male stepped forward and spoke. "So, you're giving up?"

"No," Draykon said. "When our Master dies what do you think will happen to us. I doubt the royals will simply throw us in the dungeons. They will kill us, all of us."

The two followers stood facing Draykon, thinking about what he just said and pondered his words.

"What will you do?" the male asked.

Draykon eyed the male suspiciously, not knowing whether he should reveal his plans to another follower. Before he could decide, the male follower spoke up again.

"We decided to join our Master because we were shunned by society. When the Master is gone there is nothing for us here. Take us with you and we will serve by your side," the male said.

Draykon eyed the two, thinking whether or not he should take them up on the offer to join him.

"What powers did our Master give you?" Draykon asked.

"I have been given the ability to transform into a crocodile, that is at least 17 feet long," the male replied.

Draykon nodded his approval then spoke again. "What do they call you?"

"Calix," the man replied.

"Welcome Calix," Draykon smiled deviously, then turned to the female. "And you?"

"My name is Veda, and I can turn into a vulture. The Master manly used me for scouting and spying," the female spoke.

"Interesting," Draykon said as he smiled. "Welcome Veda."

Turning around Draykon started walking again, then called over his shoulder. "Try to keep up."

Calix and Veda smiled at each other before running to catch up with Draykon.

"Where are we headed?" Calix asked.

"The nearest town," Draykon said plainly.

"Shall I scout ahead and see which one is closest?" Veda asked.

Draykon stopped and looked at Veda while thinking.

"Yes, find the closest one. I need to find a doctor," Draykon ordered.

Veda smiled and bowed before Draykon, then began transforming into a vulture. Once done she flew up over the trees and out of sight.

Draykon smiled to himself. He now had an advantage, but he needed more followers, stronger ones. He also needed to be more powerful, that way he wouldn't be defeated like his previous master, who was probably dead by now. Draykon believed that the Dark One had rushed into starting the war, instead of waiting, healing, and getting more powerful with time. Using his power to summon more creatures after the first wave made him weak, but the master wouldn't listen to Draykon. That was his mistake. If he had just waited and healed, he would have been able to use his shadow abilities to easily defeat King Nikolai, but the master was impatient.

Draykon was different. He would be patience, not making the same mistake his master did.

Flapping wings announced to Draykon and Calix that Veda hand landed on a nearby branch.

"What news do you have?" Draykon asked.

"The nearest town is Helmsdale. It's only a small town, only about 2km from here," Veda explained.

Draykon nodded his approval then spoke. "How long to the Kingdom of Zolatta from the town of Helmsdale?"

"An hour's walk or more," Veda answered.

"So, an hour's walk or if we find horses, we could reach the Zolatta docks in half that time," Draykon thought mumbling to himself. "Let's go."

CHAPTER THIRTY

*"By the sweat of your brow you will eat your food
until you return to the ground, since from it you were taken;
for dust you are and to dust you will return."*

Genesis 3:19

"Nikolai!" Juliet cried. "Nikolai."

After witnessing the defeat of the Prince of Darkness and the sacrifice Nikolai had made, Issac rushed over to tell Juliet what had happened. Following the distraught Juliet, Issac and Queen Julia rushed to the scene to find Juliet in tears. She was frantically healing Nikolai's stomach wound, while blood continued to pour out from him. Queen Julia instructed Issac to use cloths to put pressure on Nikolai's wound to prevent any more blood loss, while Juliet and herself continued to heal him at rapid speed. Juliet could hear the voices of her friends coming up from behind her, but didn't stop to acknowledge them as she kept on healing her husband. Nix continued to whine with worry for his master as he sat close to Juliet.

"Lieutenant Riley," Issac said.

"Yes sir," she replied standing before him.

"Is anyone in charge down there?" Issac said, nodding towards their camp.

"Yes, King Jabari has ordered the wounded to be taken to the tent. The volunteers are down there working. They will let Queen Julia know if anyone is critical. Princess Iris is instructing her animals to help with clearing the battlefield, while the alicorn's are helping our fallen comrades," Lieutenant Riley explained.

"Good, keep me informed," Issac instructed.

"Of course, sir," Lieutenant Riley said, before leaving to check in with the others.

Juliet was glad that everyone was working together as a team while she focused on Nikolai. She could see that her mother was getting weak from healing, as she was feeling the same, but she wouldn't stop.

"Mother I can-," Juliet began.

"No. I'm fine. I want to help," Queen Julia said, insisting.

"Thank you," Juliet whispered between tears.

After a while of healing, Juliet and her mother breathed a sigh of relief as they both saw that the bleeding had stopped. Juliet looked to her husband's chest and rejoiced as she saw it rise and fall as he began to breath properly again, but he was still unconscious and grimacing in pain. Juliet continued to heal him with the help of her mother. After several more minutes, his wounds were completely healed. Nikolai then slowly opened his eyes and looked around. Friends and family surrounded him and were relieved to see he was alive. Nikolai moved his hand weakly towards Juliet and she took his hand tenderly.

"Hey," Nikolai whispered back.

"Hi," she whispered, kissing his hand.

"I love you," he whispered.

"I love you too," Juliet replied.

Juliet and Queen Julia moved back as Nikolai slowly sat up with the help of Issac. Nikolai smiled as he looked around at his family and friends. Looking past the group, Nikolai inspected the last place he saw the Prince of Darkness turn to dust.

"For dust you are and to dust you will return," Oberon quoted from the Tanakh.

"Amen," Nikolai agreed weakly.

Nikolai smiled at his wife and kissed her, relieved to be alive and to have conquered the Prince of Darkness, and his army of dark creatures and followers. Now there would be peace within the four kingdoms again.

✦ ✦ ✦ ✦ ✦

A few weeks later.

King Nikolai stood in front of a large crowd just outside the palace with Juliet by his side. The townspeople were all gathered around to hear the current news regarding the Prince of Darkness and the war. There had been rumours and talk amongst townspeople about the outcome, but Nikolai had yet to reveal all the details.

After coming home from war, Juliet had put Nikolai on bed rest after his near-death experience, and had asked Theo to help her run the kingdom. She had briefly given a speech to the people but promised more news once Nikolai had recovered. Now standing in front of the crowd Nikolai felt overwhelmed. Juliet reached for her husband's hand and squeezed it reassuringly. Nikolai smiled back at her then cleared his throat.

"Thank you for all coming out today. Today we celebrate the defeat of the Prince of Darkness, his followers, and his creatures." He paused for a moment while the townspeople cheered at the news. "We mourn for those who fought in this battle and lost their lives, and we pray for their loved ones during this time of grieving. Help is available for those who need it. We are here to support and to help one another, as we work together for a peaceful future for all. Thank you."

Juliet clapped along with the crowd as they hailed their King and Queen, smiling as she thought about the future and what it held for them both.

The End

CHARACTER INDEX

King Nikolai - King of Zolatta, wife is Juliet. Wields a sword with the topaz Gem in the swords hilt.

Queen Juliet - Queen of Zolatta, husband is Nikolai. Has the sapphire healing Gem and the emerald earth Gem.

Theo - Advisor and friend to the King of Zolatta.

Fitzwilliam - Brother to Theo, works as a blacksmith.

Lord Hain - Lord of Silverwood and Finnick's father. Previous Captain of the Royal Guard. Wields a sword and axe.

Queen Julia - Queen of Elaxon and Juliet's mother. Holds the sapphire healing Gem.

Captain Issac - Captain of the Royal Guard of Elaxon.

Queen Nala - Queen of Neylon. Husband is Jabari and son is Omari. Holds the ruby Gem as a ring.

King Jabari - King of Neylon. Wife is Nala and son is Omari. Holds the ruby Gem in his sword.

Prince Omari - Prince of Neylon. Cursed by the Dark One to transform into a griffin. Holds the ruby Gem in his gauntlets on both arms.

Queen Athena - Queen of Kudzu. Daughter is Iris. Holds the amethyst Gem as a crown.

Princess Iris - Princess of Kudzu. Holds the amethyst Gem as a crown.

Finnick - 1st Lieutenant from the Kingdom of Zolatta. Wields an axe and daggers. Father is Lord Hain.

Jarreth - 2nd Lieutenant from the Kingdom of Zolatta. Wields a bow and arrow and daggers. Is mute.

Captain Oberon - Captain of the Royal Guard from the Kingdom of Zolatta. Wields a broadsword.

Prince of Darkness - Evil being that wants war, destruction, and death. Is cunning and deceptive.

Claud - Follower of the Prince of Darkness. Can turn into a giant wolf.

Anna - Follower of the Prince of Darkness. Can turn into an anaconda.

Serpentina - Follower of the Prince of Darkness. Can transform into a basilisk.

The God of Light - Good being that is love and peace.

Malachi - An angel and messenger for the God of Light.

Amisha - An alicorn and a gift from the God of Light. Also belongs to Juliet and is the key in finding the Cave of Lumina.

Alvina - Leader of the alicorn's. Helps the group find the Cave of Lumina. Teaches King Nikolai how to use the Crystal Gem.

Chase - Spy/Captain of the Royal Guard from Kudzu.

Nix - A white wolf Nikolai saves in his test to obtain The Sword of The Kings in previous book. Loyal to Nikolai and Juliet.

Tanakh - Hebrew word meaning Bible.

Lucas - Young orphan boy from the kingdom of Kudzu. Jarreth and Finnick train him to fight.

Kirsten - Captain of the Royal Guard from the Kingdom of Neylon.

Ethan - 1st Lieutenant from the Kingdom of Neylon.

Lord Blackstone - Lord of Ashmore.
Loyal to the King of Zolatta.

Screechers - Cave dwellers. Small, brown, with sharp teeth. Brings victims to the Leviathan that is trapped within the Cave of Lumina.

Riley Shaw - 1st Lieutenant from the Kingdom of Elaxon.

Draykon - Follower of the Prince of Darkness.
Can transform into a Komodo Dragon.

Calix - Follower of the Prince of Darkness. Follows Draykon. Can turn into a crocodile.

Veda - Follower of the Prince of Darkness. Follows Draykon. Can turn into a vulture.

Matthew - An angel who is based off a person in the Bible.

Simon - An angel who is based off a person in the Bible.

Sally and Sam - Cave salamanders who help Princess Iris.

About the Author

My name is Lucy. I started writing when I was in high school and loved it. I haven't chosen a particular genre that I like to write about, as I'm still new at writing. But I would love to explore all genres in the future.

I also love to read books in my spare time. I can go from reading Disney one day, to horror the next, so I'm keen to give almost any book a go.

I live on the Sunshine Coast in Australia and love it. I love going for walks along the beach, and rainforest walks. This gives me time to think of good book ideas, and to be with my family and friends at the same time.

I'm a Christian who loves God, and goes to church. What I love about my church is that the people there are all so kind and welcoming. We also love to help our community. I also work part-time as a carer in aged care, as I love to help people.

Author's Notes & Acknowledgements

Hi everyone. Thank you for taking the time to read my novel. I am so happy that I was able to publish this book.

The Secrets of the Crystal Gem is a work of fiction. Any names of places mentioned in this book are all fictional.

I would like to acknowledge my sister Larissa, for giving me advice for my book, editing, and proofreading it for me. For also helping me along the way during the editing, proofreading, and publishing journey.

I would like to acknowledge Kelly, a good friend of mine. She helped me with choosing some of the creatures that are mentioned in my book. Thank you for lending me your books on mythological creatures.

I would like to acknowledge Isis, another friend of mine. She was the person who named King Nikolai and Mildred. She also created the characters, Captain Oberon, Finnick and Jarreth, their personalities, and their weapons. I'm glad she did, as I had so much fun writing about these three characters, and their strong bond that they have.

I would also like to acknowledge Jendy and Pastor Phil, who serve at Hope Community Church on the Sunshine Coast. Thank you for all the biblical references, ideas, and advice throughout the book process. Thank you for the constant prayer. God knows I needed it.

I would like to acknowledge my other sister Luana, for giving me some good names for my characters, and for also being supportive of my book writing process.

I would like to acknowledge a friend from church, Eli. All the dad jokes and Finnick's humour were inspired by him. Thanks for making us laugh with all your jokes.

I would like to thank The Book Studio in Bli Bli, for helping me throughout my publishing journey.

For those of you who loved this book and would like to see more of this universe, and its characters, let me know on Instagram or Facebook. I can happily say this will be a small series.

How to stay in touch and find other books
Facebook: Author Lucy Khan
Email: AuthorLucyKhan@gmail.com
Instagram: lucykhan1614

www.ingramcontent.com/pod-product-compliance
Lightning Source LLC
Chambersburg PA
CBHW070003120726
47909CB00003B/785